Triple Creek

Ranch

Book Three

Rustlers

Rebekah A. Morris

No part of this book may be reproduced in any form whatsoever, except for a brief quotation for review purposes only, without prior written authorization from the publisher.

Illustration Copyright © 2014 Nikola Belley

All rights reserved.

Copyright © 2014 Rebekah A. Morris

All rights reserved.

ISBN: 1500540994
ISBN-13: 978-1500540999

Read Another Page Publishing

DEDICATION

To Shannon Wedge who first asked if I was going to write three books in the Triple Creek series.

And to my best friends Angela Covington and Amber Covington Nasby. Life wouldn't have been the same without you both!

CONTENTS

1	Trouble at the Bar X	1
2	Under New Management	9
3	Ranchers' Plans	17
4	Naming the Foal	25
5	Norman Turns Lawyer	35
6	"I Can't Let Go!"	43
7	The Sunday School Picnic	53
8	Fiddling Around with a Rattlesnake	61
9	New Deputies	71
10	Greg's Return	79
11	Patient Help	87
12	Pranksters or Rustlers?	95
13	A Big Mistake	103
14	"Send Him Soon"	111
15	A New Mavrich	119
16	Dreary Weather	129
17	Twisted Fences	137
18	Mysterious Riders	145
19	A Gamble	155

20	A Double Job	163
21	Missing Hands	171
22	Unable to Love	181
23	Trailing Thieves	191
24	Settling Scores	201
25	Tying Up Loose Ends	211

Chapter 1

TROUBLE AT THE BAR X

"Mr. Mavrich!"

Norman Mavrich turned quickly from the corral as the shout and the sound of pounding hooves thundering down the lane alerted him to trouble. "That looks like Elbert Ledford from the Bar X!" he exclaimed to Jim Hardrich, the foreman of Triple Creek Ranch, and Lloyd Hearter, the youngest hand. "Wonder what's gotten him so upset?"

There was no time for either man to reply before the excited rider had reined in his foam covered horse before them.

"What's wrong, Elbert?" Norman asked sharply, stepping up beside his visitor and noticing the young man's pale face and the rapid breathing of both horse and rider.

"It's Pa . . . rustlers . . . hands left . . . accused 'em . . . ranch . . . no one . . . cattle . . ."

"Whoa, slow down a bit there, Ledford. Now, just dismount, get a hold of yourself and then tell us what's going on. Here Hearter," Mavrich directed, after the rider had slid to the ground, passing the reins of the exhausted horse to his ranch hand. "Take care of the horse."

Lloyd nodded and led the horse slowly towards the barn. He was curious to know what was going on the the Bar X but knew better than to argue with the ranch boss.

"Lloyd," a gentle voice called from the porch of the

house. "Who just rode in?"

"Lloyd looked up. "Elbert Ledford did, Mrs. Mavrich. He looks about done in too."

Jenelle Mavrich nodded and slipped inside.

Back at the corral, Elbert was slowly catching his breath and making a second attempt to tell his troubles. "We had rustlers at our place last night," he began, taking off his hat and running his fingers through his hair. "We found we were missing twenty-five head this morning."

Hardrich let out a whistle. "Twenty-five head in one night!"

"Well, I reckon it's been going on more than last night, but no one's had time to check. Pa got real angry over the whole thing. I've never seen him so worked up. Why he . . . he . . ." Elbert turned away and rested his elbows on the rail fence of the corral, his sentence unfinished.

Norman exchanged quick glances with Hardrich before placing a hand on the young man's shoulder. "What happened, Ledford?"

Elbert didn't turn around and his voice was low. "He accused the men of stealing the cattle themselves. Everyone denied it, and then Pa fired our foreman and the others quit, except Cook. Pa collapsed right after that. Edgar and I were able to get him to bed. Now Edgar's gone for the doc and I . . . I didn't know who else to turn to, so—"

"You came to the right place, Elbert," Norman interrupted, squeezing his shoulder. "I'll ride back with you."

"Would any of you care for a glass of cool water?"

Norman turned to find his wife standing beside him with a pitcher and three glasses. "You shouldn't be carrying those," he scolded gently, taking the tray from her hands. "But I will say that a glass of water is just what we need. Here Elbert," Mr. Mavrich had filled a glass and held it out to his guest. "There's been trouble at the Bar X, Jenelle," Norman explained before draining his own glass of water.

"You are going to help, aren't you?"

"I don't think he could do anything else, Mrs.

Mavrich," Hardrich smiled. "He just wasn't made that way."

For a moment Mr. Mavrich stood deep in thought. At last he looked up. "Hardrich, I'm going to take Hearter with me. His horse is one of the fastest we've got and there's no knowing if we might need help."

"Mr. Mavrich," Elbert began, "I don't think my horse is up for much more of that kind of riding. You see I rode him in from the range this morning when we found out about the cattle missing and then it was a hard ride here and . . ."

"Don't worry about it. You can leave him here and ride one of our mounts. Hardrich, get Apache saddled for him. I'll get Captain ready." The two men hurried off to the barn leaving Elbert and Jenelle waiting.

"How is your mother doing, Elbert?" Jenelle asked quietly. "I couldn't help overhearing about your father."

Staring up at the fleecy white clouds floating along in the spring sky, the young man drew a long breath. "She was calm when I left, Mrs. Mavrich. I left Cook with her, and Elvira's at school. Maybe I shouldn't have left them alone. What if something happens? I've got to get right back! I don't know what I was thinking to leave no one at the ranch with her but Cook!" His voice was growing more excited and he bit his trembling lower lip. "If anything happens and I'm not there—"

"Now wait a minute, Elbert," Jenelle said gently, placing a soft hand on his arm. "You were doing what you thought was best. The Lord hasn't left your mother. Or," she added softly, "your father."

For a moment he leaned against the corral fence, his eyes closed and his shoulders tense. Then he sighed. Looking up he said, "Thank you, Mrs. Mavrich."

Neither one said another word, for Norman, Hardrich and Lloyd came up then with the horses. Quickly kissing Jenelle, Mr. Mavrich swung up on his horse and said, "I don't know how long I'll be gone, Jenelle, but don't worry."

She smiled and waved as the three horses started down the lane at a brisk trot. Picking up the tray with its empty pitcher and glasses, Jenelle asked, "Isn't the Bar X the second ranch that has been hit by rustlers this spring?"

The foreman nodded grimly. "Yep, and I don't think it'll be the last time either. Rustlers never stop unless they're caught. I'll be out in the pasture if you need me, Mrs. Mavrich." And the older man walked away with determined strides.

The three men rode along at a steady, ground-eating canter. Elbert wanted to move faster but Mr. Mavrich, sensing it, reached out a hand and placed it on his younger companion's arm. "Don't push the horses, Ledford," he advised. "We may need to do some fast riding later and spent horses won't do any good. Besides, if Edgar went for the doctor, they are probably already back at the ranch."

Though he still felt impatient, Elbert could see the wisdom of Mr. Mavrich's words and refrained from kicking Apache into a mad gallop.

Seeking to help divert his troubled thoughts, Lloyd leaned forward on his horse to ask, "How long have you folks been living on the Bar X?"

"It'll be five years come summer."

"Where'd you live before that?"

"Chicago."

Norman gave a low whistle. "Your pa sure knew how to turn his hand to ranch life in a short time! Coming from Chicago to a ranch is quite a change."

Quickly Elbert shook his head. "Oh, no. Pa's been a ranch hand most of his life. That's how he knows the business so well. You see," he added, noticing the confused looks of his companions, "Pa came out to Chicago about seven years ago and met Mother. They were married almost a year later. Elvira was only six at the time. Our father had died not quite two years before from an illness. Pa tried to like it in the city, for Mother's sake, I believe, but at last he couldn't stand it any longer and moved us all out here. It was quite a change at first, but Edgar and I have grown to like it. I'm not sure about Elvira."

"What about your mother," Lloyd asked. "Does she like it out here?"

Elbert shook his head. "I couldn't say for sure. I think she does."

Several miles passed without the three riders saying another word then, as they neared the Bar X, they unconsciously nudged their mounts into a fast pace.

"I don't know what we're going to do if Pa's laid up for long," Elbert sighed.

"Don't borrow trouble," Mr. Mavrich advised as they turned into the Bar X lane and saw the doctor's rig out front.

Reining up by the door, Elbert flung himself off his horse and dashed into the house, leaving his companions to do what they would.

Norman didn't blame the young man. He'd felt the same way when Uncle Hiram had become ill. Turning to his young hand, he said, "Come on. Let's take the horses around and give them a drink and loosen their saddles. I don't want to do anything till I hear how Mr. Ledford is."

Twenty minutes later Elbert joined them at the barn with his younger brother.

"How is he?" Mr. Mavrich asked quickly.

Elbert shook his head. "Doc said it was his heart. He's resting right now, but Doc says he won't be up and about for several weeks and then he'll have to take things easy. I don't know what we're going to do!" And he sat down on the tail of the wagon which stood beside the barn.

"Who was your foreman?"

"Clint Johnson."

Norman nodded. "Good man. He worked for my uncle several years back. Did he say where he was going?"

Edgar spoke up. "I saw him in town when I went for the doc."

"Any other hands with him?"

Edgar nodded. "I saw several."

"Good." He turned to the oldest son. "Elbert, with your pa laid up you have a choice, you can either call it quits, sell your cattle and give up, or you can rise to the place of ranch boss until he's well enough to take over again. Which is it going to be?"

Before Elbert had a chance to reply, a soft, feminine voice answered for him. "Elbert is going to take over the ranch. I know he can do it."

The men turned to see Mrs. Ledford.

"Mother," Elbert sprang from the wagon and started forward anxiously, "is he—"

"He's resting and Dr. French is with him. But Son, this is our only home and you will have to take over now." She looked up at her tall son steadily.

"But I don't know—" he began and stopped. Drawing a deep breath, he turned from his mother's eyes to Mr. Mavrich. "Mr. Mavrich, could you . . . I know you're busy, but—"

"I'm never too busy to help someone," Norman replied quietly and held out his hand.

Mrs. Ledford smiled as she watched her sons shake hands with Mr. Mavrich. "I must return to the house now," was all she said, but her face looked peaceful and the smile remained on her lips as she turned to go.

"What should we do first, Mr. Mavrich?" And Elbert turned from watching his mother disappear into the house.

Norman was quick in replying, for he knew of several things that needed to be done. "Are you willing to hire Johnson back? And will you take the hands that quit?"

"If you think we should."

"I do."

Edgar spoke up. "I don't think they'll come back after Pa fired Johnson and accused them all of stealing."

"Leave that to me," Norman said. "Are you sure twenty-five head is all you're missing?"

"Yes. We don't have a large herd like you do, sir, and Johnson knew just how many we had including calves."

"All right. You both know where the cattle are? Are they all in one area? Good. Edgar, Hearter, ride out to the cattle and keep an eye on things. Lloyd," he turned to his young hand, "keep your eyes open for any signs of rustlers or where they might have gotten in." He turned quickly to Elbert. "Has anyone ridden the fence this morning?"

Elbert shook his head. "We hadn't gotten to that yet when the missing cattle were discovered and the trouble began."

For a moment Norman Mavrich stared out at the empty pasture near the barn. "Think you can move the cattle to a closer pasture?"

"If we have help."

"Decide on one and go ride fence on it. It wouldn't do to put your cattle in a pasture with a broken fence. And make sure you have your rifles with you." He looked at Elbert and Edgar. "I hope you won't need them, but if rustlers think there's no one here, they may be back. Now you cattlemen had better get going. I'm heading to town."

The three young men were soon on their way out towards where the cattle were grazing. For a moment Norman stood watching them over the back of Captain's saddle. Then with a sigh he tightened the cinch and putting his foot in the stirrup, swung up into the saddle. "Come on, Captain," he turned his horse's head. "Let's go get a foreman and some hands."

Riding into Rough Rock, Norman caught sight of the sheriff and hailed him.

Sheriff Hughes turned and recognizing the horse and rider, started towards them. "What are you doing in town this afternoon, Mavrich?" he questioned looking up at the rider.

"There's been trouble at the Bar X. Have you heard?"

The sheriff shook his head. "I noticed there were more men in the saloon than usual for this time of day in the middle of the week, but I hadn't heard anything. What's up?"

"The Bar X was hit last night. They lost twenty-five head. Ledford lost his temper, fired Johnson and, after the rest of the hands quit, had a fit. Doc said it's his heart, and he'll be in bed for a few weeks at least."

"Who's running the ranch?"

"Elbert will if he can get some help. I came to find Johnson."

"Who's out at the ranch now?"

"Elbert, Edgar and Hearter."

The sheriff nodded. "I reckon Johnson's in the saloon. While you're talking to him I'll go saddle up and ride back with you. Those rustlers have got to be stopped."

"They will be if they ever try working Triple Creek," Norman promised darkly, nudging Captain down the street to the saloon.

Johnson wasn't in the saloon, just sitting on the porch, when Norman dismounted and looped the reins around the hitching post.

"Norman Mavrich," Johnson exclaimed, standing up and holding out his hand. "Am I glad to see you. Say, Triple Creek isn't hiring anyone right now by any chance?"

"No, but I have a job for you." Norman replied. "Elbert Ledford is offering you a job as foreman at the Bar X."

CHAPTER 2

UNDER NEW MANAGEMENT

Johnson snorted. "In case you hadn't heard, Mavrich, I just got fired from there."

"I heard. But you were fired by Mr. Ledford. He's had a fit and won't be out of his bed for weeks Doc said, so Elbert is taking over. He needs a good foreman. Will you do it?"

For a minute Johnson thought. "All right. I'll go back. But not one of the hands was involved with the cattle rustling."

"I'll take your word on that. Now, can you find some good hands? I don't know how many you need for the Bar X, but I reckon you do."

"Sure, I can find them. How soon are we wanted?"

"Just as soon as you can get there."

"All right." Clint Johnson stepped to the door of the saloon and called a few men. Speaking in low tones to them for several minutes, the men nodded and followed Johnson across the porch and to the horses tied in front of the livery. "You heading back to the Bar X, Mavrich?"

Mounting Captain, Norman nodded and started down the street. "The sheriff's coming too," he said. "He's getting his horse."

When the sheriff arrived moments later, the whole group headed towards the Bar X ranch at a rapid pace while Norman filled them in on what was happening.

Johnson shook his head. "I wouldn't have left if he hadn't dismissed me. Maybe I shouldn't have gone even then."

The sheriff asked some questions of the men as they rode, and before long the barns of the Bar X came into sight. The men dismounted and Norman briefly outlined some instructions and sent the hands off, some to find Elbert, send him back and take over riding fence on the new pasture, and the others to start bringing the cattle in. Sheriff Hughes rode off with the latter group to look for signs of the thieves.

"Johnson," Norman said, turning to the Bar X foreman after the other had ridden off, "I don't mean to take over this ranch. After all, you probably know the ways and workings of it better than I could in so short a time, but Elbert was too upset to think about much."

Before Norman could say any more, Johnson held up his hand. "Skip it, Mavrich. Truth is, I'm glad you're here. Ledford's ways aren't like your uncle's were on the Triple Creek. There a man was expected to think for himself and use his own judgment about many things and in an emergency. Not here. I'm almost afraid to try thinking on my own again."

Norman Mavrich snorted. "Well, it's time you did. No wonder Elbert didn't know where to start! You're going to have to help him. Now I suggest we unsaddle these horses and give them a rest. After Elbert comes we can go over some plans."

When the young man did arrive, Norman began making suggestions and asking questions that forced Johnson and Elbert to take an active part in planning the work for the next few days.

"I'll lend you Hearter for a few days or one of my other hands, if you think you'll need them."

Johnson shook his head. "Once we get the cattle moved, I don't think we will. This ranch was operating with the same number it has now, with the exception of Mr. Ledford. What do you think, Elbert? Can we manage it alone?"

"I reckon we can give it a try."

Norman smiled. He could sense that Johnson was rising to the challenge and Elbert was not far behind. "I have a feeling that once the cattle are moved closer, the rustlers will shift on to other ranches. But," he added, glancing up at the sky, "it wouldn't hurt to keep a patrol out the next few nights."

"How many men should we send out each night?" Elbert inquired.

Mr. Mavrich turned to look at the young man. "I think you and Johnson can decide that. I'll be back by tomorrow if I can get away, but if you ever need me, just send someone out to the ranch. I always have time to help. Now what do you say we ride out and lend a hand with the cattle."

"I'd like to see how Mother's doing first," Elbert said quietly. "I'll ride out and join you as soon as I can."

To this Johnson and Mavrich agreed, knowing that it must be difficult for the young man to have the load of a ranch suddenly dumped on his shoulders.

It was late when Norman and Hearter rode away from the Bar X, taking Apache back with them and promising to return Elbert's horse the next day. The sun was low in the west and the busy sounds of day had changed to a quieter hush of evening. The birds twittered softly, the grasses whispered as a light breeze drifted down from the distant mountains and across the fields and pastures in the valley; even the steady plodding of the horses on the hard packed road seemed to have taken on an added quietness. Neither rider spoke for some time, each being busy with their own thoughts.

"Mr. Mavrich." Lloyd's voice at last broke the silence.

Norman turned. His young hand's face was grave and thoughtful. "Yes."

"Did you know that about the Ledfords? About Chicago and all that?"

"No. I haven't been able to get well acquainted with

Samuel Ledford. He hasn't been very social, but I have talked with Elbert several times. Why?"

Lloyd shook his head. "Just thinking." He was quiet for a long time, then in low tones he remarked, "It must have been hard." A deep sigh followed his remark and Norman was sure he was thinking about his own father's death and his mother's ill health.

"Let's remember to keep them in our prayers, Lloyd."

"Yes, sir."

It was completely dark when Norman and Lloyd arrived back at the Triple Creek; however, there were lights on in the house and in the bunkhouse.

"You want me to take care of Captain, Mr. Mavrich?" Lloyd asked as the two men dismounted.

"Here, I'll take him, sir," Scott's voice from the dark doorway of the barn gave Norman no time to reply. A lantern was lit and Scott stepped forward and took Captain's reins.

"Thanks, Scott. I should get to the house before Jenelle worries too much. Tell Hardrich I'll come by later to talk." Then he turned and hurried across the dark yard, sprang up to the porch ignoring the steps entirely and opened the kitchen door.

"Norman?"

Tossing his hat on the table Norman replied, "Yes, Jenelle, I'm home," as he quickly stepped into the dining room where he met her coming from the front room. "Sorry I'm so late, Sweet," he whispered as he embraced her tenderly.

Lifting her head, Jenelle smiled and returned her husband's kiss. "How are things at the Bar X?"

Norman opened his lips to talk, but Jenelle suddenly pulled away and said briskly, "Go wash up first, Dear, then come and eat. Mrs. O'Connor has kept your supper warm. You can tell me about the day as you eat."

Norman wasted no time in following those directions for he was hungry. It was only a few minutes before Jenelle set a plate of hot food before him and sank down into a nearby chair. "Where are Orlena and Mrs. O'Connor?" Norman asked after he had related a shortened account of the day.

"Gone to bed. Mrs. O'Connor was tired, and since tomorrow is another school day, I wouldn't let Orlena stay up, for I didn't know how long it would be before you returned."

"Perhaps you shouldn't have waited up for me either," Norman suggested softly, looking at his wife with a mixture of love and concern.

With a little laugh, Jenelle rose to take his dishes. "Nonsense. I wouldn't have been able to sleep anyway until you returned." She paused long enough to kiss him before adding as she carried the dishes to the sink, "I enjoyed the quiet evening, and the others haven't been gone very long."

Pushing back his chair, Norman rose and followed his wife into the kitchen. "I have to talk to Hardrich, Jenelle, and I don't know how long I'll be. Promise me you won't do anything but wash those dishes and go up to bed."

"All right. I promise."

"Thank you, Darling." And flashing a smile at her, Norman seized his hat and was gone.

It was nearly an hour later before Norman slipped back into the quiet house. Taking the lit lamp from the table, he made his way through the darkened house and up the stairs. Turning down the lamp to a dim glow, he softly opened the door. He hoped he hadn't awakened Jenelle, and after shutting the door, he turned to see the bed empty. A slight movement drew his eyes to his wife's rocker where he saw in the moonlight which streamed through the window, Jenelle, sitting in a warm wrapper.

"Jenelle Mavrich," he scolded gently, "I thought you promised to go to bed."

Turning her eyes from the window, Jenelle smiled. "I did. But I couldn't sleep and the light of the moon was so pretty . . . So I decided to sit here for a while." Her eyes turned back to the window.

After slipping his boots off, Norman crossed the room. "What are you thinking about?" he whispered softly, gently stroking Jenelle's long hair.

"Many things."

"What?"

"Us . . . this spring . . . Orlena . . . wondering what life will be like in a couple months, this summer . . . five, six years from now . . ." She sighed softly and rested her head back against her husband.

"Come on," Norman whispered, tenderly lifting her from the chair. "You can do the rest of your thinking in bed."

"Norman," Jenelle's hushed voice broke the stillness of the room just as Norman was about the blow out the lamp a few minutes later. "Whose fried chicken do you like better, mine or Mrs. O'Connor's?"

Turning with the lamp in his hand, Norman regarded his wife with puzzled eyes. "Why do you ask?"

"I wondered who should make it for the Sunday School picnic next Saturday. If you like mine I can make it, but I wasn't sure . . . Which *do* you like better?"

Blowing out the lamp, Norman sat down on the bed and leaned over Jenelle, "I'm not going to answer that. Now go to sleep."

"So you like Mrs. O'Connor's better? That's all right, I—"

But a finger was placed over her lips and Norman whispered with a laugh in his voice, "Go to sleep! I won't answer anything until morning."

The following morning at breakfast, Orlena listened in silence to Norman's story of the Bar X and all that had occurred on the previous day. She was silent so long after Norman finished talking that at last he asked her if something was wrong.

She shook her head. "I was just thinking. No wonder

Elvira . . ." Her voice trailed off and she stared down at her plate. "Did you see her after she returned from school?"

"No. I was probably out on the range when she arrived home. I don't know if she'll be in school today or not."

Jenelle folded her napkin and placed it on the table. "Are you going back over to the Bar X today, Norman?"

Norman nodded. "Yep. I've got to take their horse back and I want to see how they're getting on."

Looking over at Mrs. O'Connor, Jenelle hesitated and then said, "Perhaps I should ride over with you and see how Emmaline is. It must be very hard on her."

"I won't let you ride, but if you care to accompany me, we'll hitch up the light wagon or the carriage. Orlena," Norman turned to his sister who has still staring at her plate, "would you like a ride into school? Or at least a ride to town?" Taking her absentminded nod as consent, he turned to the housekeeper. "Would you like to ride along, Mrs. O'Connor?"

But Mrs. O'Connor shook her head. "'Tis not likely ye'll be needin' me along and I have work here to be doin' sure. You just be gettin' along and I'll look after the house."

Plans were thus formed and within an hour the Mavrich carriage was rolling down the lane with the Bar X horse tied along behind. No one seemed inclined to talk much and at the edge of Rough Rock, Orlena picked up her books and climbed down. "Thank you for the ride," was all she said before hurrying off down the main street.

Her thoughts were troubling as she thought about Elvira, and when Charity Hearter met her at the schoolhouse steps, there was a frown on her face.

"What's wrong, Orlena?" Charity asked. The two girls had become good friends and twice already Charity had returned to the Triple Creek with Orlena and Lloyd had taken her home again in the evening.

"Have you seen Elvira yet?" was Orlena's unexpected question.

Surprised, Charity shook her head. "No, I haven't seen

her. Why?"

"Rustlers took twenty-five head of their cattle and Mr. Ledford is very ill."

Instantly Charity's sympathies were roused. "Poor Elvira! I wish there was something we could do for her."

"She won't let me do anything," Orlena sighed. "Norman and Jenelle were going over to the Bar X this morning. I don't know if she'll be here today or not."

Charity knew Orlena was referring to Elvira and not Jenelle. Her own thoughts went back to her father's death several years before. "I wouldn't want to come if my father was ill."

Orlena sat down on the steps. "He's only her stepfather. Her real father died when she was four, I think Norman said." Her voice dropped. "I was only three when I lost both Father and Mother. I don't really remember them at all."

Before Charity could do more than squeeze her friend's hand, Connie came out of the school house and rang the bell.

That day Elvira didn't come to school and Jonah Hughes, the sheriff's eldest son, mentioned the theft of Bar X cattle. "Pa says they'll catch the rustlers sooner or later."

"Let's hope it's sooner," one of the other boys said, "before they hit any other ranches."

"I wish I were allowed to go looking for them," another remarked. "I'd sure find 'em and they wouldn't get away."

This brought some laughter and Miss Hearter quickly called for order. "Let's leave the subject of cattle thieves outside and focus now on school. Shall we?"

CHAPTER 3

RANCHERS' PLANS

It was difficult for Orlena to focus on school that day. The realization that Elvira had lost her own father gave Orlena a new feeling for her, one of mingled pity and understanding quite strange to her, and one which caused her mind to wander many times during the day.

When Miss Hearter observed her staring blankly at a simple addition problem on the blackboard, she placed a hand gently on her shoulder while she said in low tones, "Orlena, I know it's difficult to keep your mind on your work when Elvira's troubles are bothering you. We only have a few more hours. Try to pay attention."

Somewhat startled that Miss Hearter could read her thoughts so plainly, Orlena did try harder, and at last school was dismissed.

For several minutes after the other children had hurried away for their homes, Charity and Orlena remained standing near the door talking in low tones.

"What can we do?"

Orlena shook her head. "I've been trying and trying to think of something but I don't think Elvira will let me do anything. She's still mad at me for—" Stopping abruptly, Orlena bit her lip and looked down at the floor. She didn't want to tell Charity the reason for Elvira's anger.

Respecting Orlena's silence, Charity said, "I suppose

the only thing we can do is keep trying to be friends with her when she comes back."

"That's not the only thing, girls."

Orlena and Charity looked up. Neither of them had noticed Connie's approach.

"You can pray for her." She placed an arm about the shoulder of her sister and then one about Orlena. "Prayer can make a big difference in a person's life, you know."

Orlena blushed and nodded. She knew what Miss Hearter was saying was true, for she had experienced it in her own life during the winter.

"I think if you girls pray for Elvira and keep trying to be nice to her, even if she doesn't show it, I think it will help her. Now you two had better get along home. Charity, tell Mother I may be a little later since I need to stop by the store for a few things."

"All right, I'll tell her. Good bye, Orlena, see you on Sunday."

Orlena waved. "Good bye, Charity." She turned to her school teacher, "Good bye, Miss Hearter. Thank you for not scolding me today. My mind was on other things."

Miss Hearter smiled. "I know it was. Now you'd better be going before your brother and sister start to worry."

₵

After church on Sunday, as the Mavriches were crossing the yard to their buggy, Norman was hailed by a handful of ranchers.

"Mavrich!"

Addressing Jenelle as he assisted her into the carriage, Norman said, "I'll be right back." Then he turned and joined the men. "What's going on?"

"The sheriff can't catch those rustlers alone, Mavrich. I say we form ourselves into a posse and hunt them down."

Norman looked slightly surprised. "Have they hit your place again, Bates?"

Mr. Bates shook his head. "No, but that doesn't mean they won't try it again."

"Well, Mavrich," another man asked, "ya with us?"

"What does the sheriff think of this idea?"

"What's the sheriff got to do with it? It's not his cattle they're stealing."

"Now listen, Bates," Norman said, one hand resting lightly on his hip, "we can't just decide we're going to be the law ourselves. We elected Hughes as our sheriff and any posse that's riding out hunting for cattle rustlers had better have the approval of the sheriff and have at least a few men deputized to bring them in. You all know that as well as I do."

"Look, Mr. Mavrich, you an yer big ranch may be able to stand the loss of a couple dozen head a cattle, but the Lucky Shoe, she ain't that large a ranch, an' ye can't be tellin' me to just be sitting by an' lettin' some theivin' rascals rob me blind."

"Harrington's right."

"Yeah, he sure is."

"You just thinking about yourself, Mavrich?"

The murmur of disgruntled voices was growing when a new voice spoke up. "You know they've got something there, Mavrich," and Mr. Bittner pushed his way to stand before Norman. "The Silver Spur might not be as large as the Triple Creek, but I aim to help the other ranchers 'cause, though I can stand the loss of some cattle more than they can, I'm not too high up to help."

"Listen! I never said I was against the idea of rounding up some cattle rustlers." Norman's voice was low and his eyes seemed to flash a bit in the afternoon sun. "All I'm saying is that we have to work with the law and not on our own. I'd suggest we hold a meeting at one of the ranches tomorrow and make some plans with the sheriff."

The grumbling stopped and instead, murmurs of assent

were beginning to drift through the crowd of ranchers gathered about on the street.

"Mavrich has a good idea the way I see things, men," Mr. Carmond said, looking around. "And I'll offer the Running C as a meeting place for tomorrow at ten."

"I'll be there, Carmond," Norman answered. "What about the rest of you men?"

"Count me in."

"Yep."

"I'll be there." Heads nodded and the men began to drift away in small groups of twos and threes.

Just as Norman, having shaken hands with Carmond and Bittner, was turning to the carriage where his wife, Orlena and Mrs. O'Connor were waiting, Sheriff Hughes stepped up and held out his hand. "I heard what was going on, Mavrich, and I must say, I like how you handled those men. Bates is a leader. He's quick at getting followers, but he doesn't always see things the right way when he gets excited."

"I couldn't have done it if Carmond hadn't backed me up. You're coming to the meeting, aren't you Sheriff?"

"Sure thing. I'll be seeing you then." Touching his hat to the ladies in the carriage, the sheriff strode off to join his family in their homeward walk.

Clicking to the horses, Norman shook the reins and the carriage rolled down the road.

"What meeting is happening tomorrow, Norman?" Jenelle asked as they left Rough Rock behind.

"A meeting to figure out some way to catch the rustlers before the other ranches get hit. Carmond offered the Running C as the meeting place."

"Well, I hope you can catch them," Jenelle agreed warmly. "It's hard on the ranchers to lose their livestock."

"We haven't had rustlers in these parts for years," Norman sighed. "It may be a while before we can catch them if they stick around."

Orlena leaned forward from the back seat of the carriage to ask, "What do they do with the cattle, Norman?"

Cattle rustling was something new and entirely different than anything she had known about in the city.

"Oh, they may butcher them and sell the meat, or they may drive the cattle some place else to sell them."

"Oh." Orlena sat back and was silent the rest of the way home.

It wasn't until the family was seated at the table that Orlena, who had been toying with her food instead of eating, suddenly turned to her brother and asked, "Norman, what if they come to Triple Creek?"

"Who? The rustlers? We'll make them wish they hadn't tried it, that's what."

"You mean you'd shoot them?"

"If necessary."

"What if you know them?"

Norman looked up, his fork half way to his mouth. "Know them?" For a moment he stared at his sister and then turned to look at Mrs. O'Connor and Jenelle. At last, laying down his fork, he said, "Orlena, what are you talking about? How could I know them? If I did, I'd tell the sheriff."

"No," Orlena shook her head. "I mean, what if you know them but didn't know they were stealing cattle. Would you still shoot them?"

"Not if I didn't have to. Orlena, I never shoot anyone unless I'm given no other choice. Now suppose you finish eating." He smiled and picked up his fork again.

Leaning against one of the posts on the porch, Jenelle pushed back a strand of hair from her face. She was tired. It was a good tired, however, and Jenelle looked with satisfaction at the clean clothes snapping gaily in the spring breeze. Mrs. O'Connor hadn't let her wash a thing that morning, but, after Lloyd had been pressed into service and carried the basket of wet laundry outside for her, Jenelle had hung up each garment. She smiled and ran a hand lightly over the front of her dress. It was a lovely spring day and Jenelle hesitated about going back inside. She didn't want to sit and

Triple Creek Ranch

sew, and Mrs. O'Connor had everything running so smoothly that Jenelle knew she wouldn't be missed if she took a walk.

"I'll just go down and see Minuet for a few minutes," she decided, stepping off the porch and slowly crossing the yard while her gaze took in the vast green ranch lands and the distant hazy mountains.

"Good morning, Mrs. Mavrich," a cheerful voice greeted her as she approached the open barn door.

"Why, Scott, I didn't know you were still here. Why aren't you out with the others?"

The ranch wrangler smiled. "Lady dropped her foal this morning out in the far pasture and Hardrich had me bring them in and settle them in the barn."

"Lady?" Jenelle looked surprised. "I didn't know she was so close to her time."

"She was a little early, that's why I brought them in. Would you like to see them?" Mrs. Mavrich's love of horses was well known on the ranch.

"Yes, I would. I thought I'd go out to the pasture and see Minuet, but I'd like to see Lady and her baby. By the way, what is it?"

"A filly, ma'am." And Scott led the way into the barn.

In the dim stall, where the spring sunshine was filtering in through the windows and open door, stood Lady, and Jenelle gently rubbed her nose before stepping closer and looking in. "Oh, Lady," she breathed, as she caught sight of the tiny, light form nuzzling her mother's side, its spindly legs seeming too thin to support even its small body.

Turning her head, Lady nuzzled her daughter and made soft noises of pride.

"Scott, she's beautiful," Jenelle whispered, moving slowly away from the stall door.

The young wrangler nodded. "She sure is. Do you have a name for the little thing?" Jenelle was the one who often came up with names for the horses born on Triple Creek.

Slowly walking out into the sunshine, Jenelle thought. At last she said, "I think I'll let Orlena name this one, if she wants to. It's the first foal this spring and it should be something special." She looked up at the ranch hand beside her. "Are you going back to the others soon?"

"Yes, ma'am, unless you have something that you need help with, or Mr. Mavrich comes back. Is there anything?" he asked.

Mrs. Mavrich shook her head. "No, I can't think of anything. Lloyd was here earlier and carried the wet laundry out for us. But suppose you go up to the house and ask Mrs. O'Connor if she needs help with anything before you leave again." She gave a little laugh as she looked back towards the house. "She won't let me do much today. And, Scott," Jenelle added as the young man turned away, "tell her I'll be out visiting with Minuet if she wants me."

The ranch hand touched his hat as he replied, "Yes, ma'am." But he remained where he was for a moment, watching the mistress of Triple Creek stroll across the yard to the corral where the pretty chestnut was grazing.

Upon reaching the fence, Jenelle leaned against a post and called softly, "Here, Minuet. That's my girl," as the horse, lifting her head, started forward with the light steps which had caused her christening.

For several minutes Jenelle stood where she was, talking to the horse and stroking its face and neck. "Don't worry," she told her. "Soon Norman will have you ready to join the rest of the horses and you'll be doing regular work with the cattle . . . I wonder if you'll be able to match Spitfire when it comes to cutting . . . Lady had a filly today. What do you think of that?" When the horse snorted and shook her head, Jenelle laughed. "You silly thing, there's no need to be jealous. You're still young. In a few years you can have a baby of your own to make a fuss over."

Minuet's ears pricked up and she lifted her head, looking down the lane.

Turning, Jenelle saw and recognized her husband on his favorite horse. With a final pat for Minuet, she hurried back towards the barn to meet the approaching rider.

Reining up and dismounting, Norman strode over to his wife. "Jenelle, what were you doing all the way over at the pasture?"

Smiling, Jenelle lifted her face for his kiss before replying, "Visiting Minuet. Mrs. O'Connor won't let me do much of anything today, so—"

"Well, I'm glad she won't!" was Norman's emphatic interruption. "You shouldn't be doing too much."

Quickly changing the subject, Jenelle said, as Norman began unsaddling Captain, "Scott just brought in Lady and her foal."

Norman turned. "Lady? Isn't it a bit early for her?"

"He said it was, but she's such a pretty little thing. You should see them."

"I will when I take Captain in." He smiled. "Have you named the—?"

"Filly," Jenelle supplied, but shook her head. "No, I thought perhaps Orlena might like to name her since she is the first foal this spring."

Lifting the saddle off, Norman replied, "Fine idea. I'm glad you thought of it. Now why don't you go on into the house, Sweetheart. I'll be along in a few minutes."

CHAPTER 4

NAMING THE FOAL

Seated at the kitchen table a quarter of an hour later, Norman told his wife and Mrs. O'Connor about the meeting over at the Running C. "Bates and a few others were for getting together a posse and starting forth on an all out search, but this time of year is difficult to leave the ranches without a good reason and a certain place to look. Right now there isn't anything to go off of. There has been no sign of rustlers since the Bar X was hit last week, and by now that trail is cold. We'll wait and watch until they strike again."

"You think they will?" Jenelle asked softly.

Norman nodded. "They haven't had any problems yet, so I reckon they're still around."

Mrs. O'Connor shook her head. "'Tis a busy an' excitin' life you live entirely, Norman Mavrich. It's not a wonder your grandmother never came out here to visit her brother."

Norman laughed. "Yes, I can't picture Grandmother enjoying this life any more than I'd enjoy being the city lawyer she always thought I should be."

"You can argue well," Jenelle remarked.

Giving a snort, Norman drained the last of his coffee and pushed back his chair. "Thanks, but I'll take cattle over a court room any day! But I can't sit around all afternoon chatting with you lovely ladies," he said, rising. "I have work to do. Jenelle, get some rest. You look tired." Stooping, he kissed his wife, smiled at the housekeeper, and then stepped outside putting his hat on as he went.

Watching him, Jenelle sighed. "I think I will lie down and rest, Mrs. O'Connor, just as soon as I help you with the dishes."

But Mrs. O'Connor would not hear of Mrs. Mavrich doing anything but going up to bed, and after a feeble protest, Jenelle gave up trying to help and moved slowly up to her room.

"Elvira was in school today," Orlena remarked that evening as she sat in the front room with her brother, sister-in-law and Mrs. O'Connor. In her lap was the beginnings of a quilt and she studied it with a frown on her face.

"Well?"

Orlena glanced up. Norman and Jenelle were both looking at her with expectant faces. "Nothing unusual happened. Elvira still won't let anyone be friends with her. I don't know why."

"Remember what you were like, Sis," Norman said softly, "when you first started school."

Orlena frowned again. "I know, but I just came from the city. Elvira's been out here for four years!"

"Could it be that she is still refusing the Help you accepted?" Jenelle's voice was quiet.

"Maybe." With a sigh, Orlena settled herself more comfortably and began sewing, the frown still upon her face. At last she asked into the silence of the room, "Do you think she'll be at the Sunday School picnic on Saturday?"

"Why don't you ask her?"

Lifting thoughtful eyes to her brother, Orlena tucked one foot under her and said, "I think I will."

"Oh, by the way, Orlena," Norman leaned back in his chair to say, "Lady had her foal this morning and Jenelle has left the naming of it to you."

For a moment Orlena just stared at her brother. A foal? She was to name it? Suddenly she sprang from her seat, scattering tiny quilt squares in every direction, and rushed across the room to hug her sister. "Oh, thank you!" she exclaimed. "Can I see it now? What does it look like? Is it a boy or a girl? I've never named anything before except my dolls. Oh, Norman," she added, whirling around to him, "can't we go out and see it now? Please!"

Norman laughed. "If I'd remembered it sooner we could have seen it in the day light, but I reckon it won't disturb the horses too much if we go out with a lantern now. But perhaps you should pick up those things from the floor first." He looked down at the gaily colored scraps.

Orlena didn't say a word but dropped at once to her knees and snatched at the pieces of cloth in a frantic hurry to go to the barn.

"Norman," Jenelle smiled, "don't make her pick them all up now. She's much too excited. Let her go."

With a grin which showed his entire agreement, he said, "All right, Sis, forget those things and let's go."

Orlena needed no urging and Jenelle's call to put on something warm, went unheard.

A moment later Orlena stood shivering with excitement outside the barn as Norman opened the door and lit a lantern. "Come on," he beckoned softly, leading the way.

A few gentle nickers sounded and some rustling of straw came from some of the dark stalls as Norman and Orlena entered the quiet barn. Straight to Lady's stall they went where Norman slid back the latch and, holding up the lantern, nodded for Orlena to enter.

"Oh," she breathed as she caught her first glimpse of the little foal lying curled up in the straw. "May I . . . may I touch it?"

"I don't think Lady will mind if you are slow and gentle," was the quiet answer.

Tiptoeing farther into the stall, Orlena sank down beside the light form and, reaching out a hand, gently rubbed the foal's neck. "Oh, Lady," she whispered, as the horse, turning to see that all was well with her baby, quizzically pushed her nose against Orlena's hand, "your baby is the most beautiful baby anywhere!"

Lady quite agreed with her and gave a snort as though saying, "Of course she is. Who could say otherwise?"

"Come on, Orlena," Norman called softly. "I think we should leave them alone now. You can name her anything you'd like."

Rising to her feet, her eyes shining with wonder and delight, Orlena moved out into the aisle as Norman shut and latched the stall door behind her and the two of them walked out of the barn together. Walking as though in a daze, Orlena didn't hear Norman's question or see his amused look at her silence, as they returned to the house and the front room.

As they entered, Jenelle turned. "Well?" she asked quickly. "Did you think of a name? Isn't she beautiful?"

There was no answer. Orlena moved slowly across the room and dropped down onto the sofa, unaware that she was sitting on her quilt. Something of the wonder and awe over a new birth seemed to have taken possession of her tongue, for she sat in absolute silence staring off into space.

Even Jenelle's questioning of Norman about what had happened, his light replies and Mrs. O'Connor's voice beside her failed to rouse Orlena's attention.

"We might as well send her up to bed," Norman chuckled, watching his young sister's face. "I don't think she'd notice anything right now." At his wife's nod of agreement, Norman raised his voice and said, "Orlena, why don't you head to bed. There's no need for you to stay up any longer."

In a dazed manner, Orlena rose and, without a word, wandered out of the room and up the stairs.

"I hope she can find her room," Norman chuckled again. "I've never seen her so speechless and utterly absorbed before. Have you Mrs. O'Connor?"

"I can't be sayin' as I have, but there are a good many things that I have never seen the child do before she came to live here."

When Jenelle softly opened Orlena's door before following Norman to their room, she discovered Orlena lying in bed, her lamp still lit, staring at the ceiling. "Good night, Orlena," Jenelle whispered softly. Then she blew out the light.

It was quite a while before Orlena seemed to come back to herself. "A horse to name," she breathed. "One I can name myself. I wonder if Norman would let me . . . She is such a beautiful thing! She just lay there dreaming. I wonder— That's it!" Orlena sat up suddenly. "What was that song I heard when Grandmother and I attended the concert . . ." For a full five minutes Orlena remained sitting deep in thought. "Beautiful dreamer? I think that was it!"

Springing from her bed and completely forgetting how late it must be, she rushed from her room, down the hall and into her brother's room. "Norman!" she called. "Jenelle! I thought of it!"

Starting up from a sound sleep, Norman demanded, "Orlena, what is wrong?" He sat up quickly.

"Nothing! I thought of a name for her."

Still groggy, Norman ran a hand over his face and asked, "A name for who? Orlena Mavrich, what on earth are you talking about? It's the middle of the night!"

"The horse, Norman. Lady's baby!"

Pushing herself up beside her husband, Jenelle asked before Norman could say anything, "What name is that?"

"Beautiful Dreamer! Isn't it the perfect name?" And Orlena clasped her hands together. "It just came to me a minute ago when I was—"

"It's a lovely name, Dear," Jenelle interrupted gently. "But why don't you go on back to bed now. You can tell us all about it in the morning." Jenelle's voice was soft and pleasant. She knew how delightful it was to think of a perfect name and also that sharing your excitement in anything was natural.

"All right. Good night!" Her dismissal didn't bother the

white clad figure in the least and the sound of her light feet dancing across the hall could be heard in the stillness.

With a deep sigh, Norman fell back onto his pillow. "Why did she have to come and wake us up just to tell us a foal's name?" he muttered with a groan.

Jenelle's soft laugh and gentle kiss was the only answer he got.

The following morning Orlena could hardly wait to get to school. She wanted to tell Charity all about Beautiful Dreamer. "Couldn't I bring Charity home with me after school to see the foal? Please," she begged. "And can't I ride Anything to school today? We'll be able to get back home so much quicker if I do." Her grey eyes moved anxiously from Jenelle to Norman, waiting for one of them to speak.

"I certainly don't mind if Charity comes over," Jenelle began, "but what about getting her back home?" She looked over at Norman. "Can you spare Lloyd for that?"

Slowly Norman nodded thoughtfully. "I reckon I can today," he said.

Scarcely waiting for him to finish his sentence, Orlena rushed around the table to thank him with a quick embrace before flying from the room, calling back over her shoulder as she went, "I only have to get my books and then I'll be ready."

Shaking his head, Norman stood up. "In that case I reckon I'd better get Anything saddled. We wouldn't want our sister late for school."

Jenelle laughed at his bewildered expression and turned back to finish her breakfast, remarking to Mrs. O'Connor, "Things have certainly been interesting around here lately." Then she sighed, "Spring. There is just something about this time of year that . . . Don't you feel it too, Mrs. O'Connor?"

"Indeed and I do."

A few moments later and Orlena set off for school on Anything, eager to tell Charity about the new little horse which she had named.

"Jenelle!" Norman's voice called soon after. "I'm heading out to the Bar X to see how things are there." He stepped up on the porch and opened the kitchen door. "Elbert asked me if I could stop by sometime, and Hardrich can take care of things around here today. I don't know when I'll be home, but don't wait up for me if I should be late."

Turning a rather anxious face to her husband, Mrs. Mavrich asked, "Are you going alone?"

"No, I'm taking Burns with me. Hardrich will have the others out with him." He hesitated. "Do you want me to leave one of the hands near by? There is work around the barn and yards that could be done."

With a smile Jenelle shook her head. "I wasn't worried about Mrs. O'Connor and me, I was thinking about you being alone if the rustlers are still around."

"Don't fret, Sweet, we'll be careful. Lloyd knows to be back in time to take Charity home this evening." Looking down into his wife's blue eyes, he added softly, "I wish I could take you with me instead of Burns."

"I wish I could go, but—"

Norman's kiss cut off the rest of Jenelle's sentence and he then turned to Mrs. O'Connor who had been busy about the kitchen. "Take care of my little wife, Mrs. O'Connor, and see that she doesn't work too hard."

"That I will, Norman Mavrich. Don't you go to fretting."

It was a lovely spring morning as Mr. Mavrich and Chad Burns set off for the Bar X. Their horses were fresh and eagerly settled into a steady lope which quickly covered the ground, and before long the Bar X ranch buildings could be seen.

"What will we be doing here, Mr. Mavrich?" Burns inquired as the two riders slowed their mounts as they neared the house.

"I'm not sure yet. Elbert didn't know I was coming out today. We may only be here a little while or it may be all day. Whoa, Captain." They had reached the barn and Norman swung down, handing the reins to his ranch hand. "I'll go up to the house and see if Mrs. Ledford can tell me where the menfolk are."

Striding across the yard, Norman's keen eyes took in many details which had gone unnoticed or pushed aside as unimportant, such as a gate that was hanging crooked, a strand of loose wire on a section of fence, and a bucket which had been kicked or had blown and was now lying under a bush. He frowned thoughtfully as he stepped onto the porch and knocked.

He didn't have to wait very long before the door was opened and Elbert stood before him looking worried, unsure and as though he hadn't slept well the night before.

"What's wrong, Elbert?" Norman asked quietly. "Is it the ranch or your father?"

After glancing quickly behind him, Elbert stepped out onto the porch, closing the door behind him. "It's both, Mr. Mavrich. Pa's upstairs trying to run the ranch from his bed, and he's had me running up and down the stairs nearly all afternoon yesterday and all this morning taking orders from his sick room to Johnson, and Johnson says he's taking orders from me, not Pa, and Pa is fuming that Doc won't let him up and—" the young man broke off and ran a hand through his hair. "To be honest, Mr. Mavrich, I don't think I can take it much longer."

CHAPTER 5

NORMAN TURNS LAWYER

"Running a ranch or your father's temper?"

"Either. Sure I want to be a rancher. I've liked it out here, but how'm I supposed to run a ranch if I'm not even sure of my own orders!"

Norman tucked a thumb in his belt and gazed about him in silence a few moments. Then he asked, "How's your mother holding up?"

Elbert looked up. "She's tired and worried about Pa."

"Is she worried about the ranch?"

"She says she's not. She has more faith in me than I have in myself."

A smile crossed Norman's face. "I think mothers are supposed to be that way. By the way, I saw the doctor's rig out front. Is he here?"

Elbert nodded. "Would you like to talk with him?"

"Yes, I think I would, when he's not busy. By the way, where are Johnson and the rest of the hands?"

"Some are riding fence and others are out with Johnson checking the cattle and working on the windmill in a far pasture." He turned and placed a hand on the door. "I'll see if Dr. French is busy right now."

Norman nodded. "I'll be along as soon as I've said a few things to Burns," and he nodded in the direction of his hand.

With a word of agreement, Elbert disappeared inside and Mr. Mavrich turned back to the barn. Burns, he noticed, hadn't been idle but had already retrieved the pail from the bush and was tightening the loose strand of wire. "Burns," he called as he approached the horses.

Quickly the hand turned from the fence and looked at his boss. "Yes sir?"

"Why don't you get these horses unsaddled. I don't think we'll be riding out to the fields, at least not for a while. Once that's done, see what you can do about, well taking care of those odd jobs that get overlooked. I see you've already started with that fence."

"I was just doing what you'd expect at the Triple Creek, sir," Burns replied, tucking his tool back in his saddlebag.

Norman nodded. "And I don't expect anything less now because it's not the Triple Creek. I've got to head inside and do some talking." With a firm clasp on the young man's shoulder, and a gentle slap on Captain's neck, Mr. Mavrich quickly returned to the house.

He let himself in and waited in the hall until Elbert and Dr. French came down the stairs.

"Good morning, Doctor," Mr. Mavrich held out his hand. "How's your patient?"

"Humph," Dr. French grunted, shaking hands. "More riled than is good for him at the moment. Go up and see if you can talk some sense into him."

"Me?" Norman shook his head. He couldn't think of anything to say to the sick and irate rancher lying in his bed.

"Please," Elbert requested quietly. "He's asking for you."

"Demanding to see you is more accurate," muttered the doctor.

For a moment Norman hesitated. On the one hand he was afraid that his visit would only infuriate the man further, but on the other, perhaps it would be good to get a few things talked over. "All right," he sighed. "If you think it will do any good." He didn't miss the look of relief which came over Elbert's face.

"I'll take you up to him."

"Elbert," the doctor said in his brusque way, "send your mother out of that sick room. Tell her I need to see her down here."

The young man nodded and, with many misgivings, Norman followed.

At the door of the sick room he paused as Elbert softly opened the door and stepped in. Norman could hear the low murmur of his voice, and a moment later Mrs. Ledford slipped from the room and said quietly, "Go on in, Mr. Mavrich."

Norman did so, and Elbert beckoned him across the room to the bed. "Pa," he said as Norman approached, "Mr. Mavrich is here."

Opening his eyes, the sick man glared at his visitor. "What do you mean by coming here and trying to take over this ranch?" he demanded hoarsely. "This ain't Mavrich land."

"No, Ledford," Norman agreed quietly, "it isn't my land and I don't aim to make it mine, but at the same time someone had to step in and lend a hand. Your son came to me and I advised him as I would have a younger brother."

"Ha!" snorted the sick man. "I know you pious types. Wait till a man's down and then undermine all his work. Well, let me tell you, Mavrich," Mr. Ladford pushed himself halfway up on one elbow, his face pale and his breathing quick. "I worked hard all my life an' I don't aim ta see you waltz in here an' steal my cattle an' my ranch! It's bad enough losin' twenty-five head a cattle and—" he stopped suddenly and a new flash came to his eyes. "I'll bet you're involved with those rustlers. I bet . . . ." he gasped for breath and his son hurried to his side.

"Pa, don't excite yourself. Lie back, please!" Gently Elbert pushed his father back onto the pillow and then, lifting his head, held a glass to his lips. "Just rest now, Pa."

But Samuel Ledford pushed him away. "No," he

gasped. "Mavrich is here and I'm going to finish what I got to say to him."

Norman moved to the other side of the bed. He gave a sigh and then said calmly, "All right, Ledford, I'll listen to what you have to say."

His words seemed to startle the sick man and for a moment he only stared at his visitor. Then he frowned. "Tryin' to make me think yer a friend. Well, it won't work. I aim ta run this ranch just like I want without any help from no one! Least of all from a rich do-gooder. Now listen here, Mavrich, I want you off my ranch an' you can take all your advice with you too. My boys don't need it. An' if any more of my cattle go missin', I'm holdin' you personally responsible. Now git!"

Throughout this tirade, Norman had stood silently by, his eyes quietly moving from the flushed and angry face on the pillow to the anxious and strained face of the son. When the sick man stopped shouting and lay glowering, Norman spoke. His voice was low, but firm. "All right, Ledford," he began, "I listened to what you had to say. Now you listen to what I have to say. No," he added quickly, raising his hand as Mr. Ledford opened his lips as though to speak. "I'm going to do the talking right now, and you might as well make up your mind to listen. I came here first because your son asked for my help. You were sick and he had a ranch to run. The only problem was, he didn't know how and all the hands were gone. You were so busy doing things your way that you never took the time to teach either son how to run a ranch. When I came, Elbert, as the eldest, had a choice to make. He could either give up the ranch or take over himself. His mother told him to take over. Well, Ledford, he has. I've offered some advice when he asked for it, but right now you are the one who is trying to ruin the ranch. You can't run it from this bed! And until you can once again be up and about, I'd advise you to turn everything over to Elbert. He's a fine young man with a good head on his shoulders, if he's allowed to use it. And if you'd quit fussing and stewing over what's going on, you'd be out of this bed a whole lot faster."

For several minutes after Norman finished, no one said a word. The Doctor, having come in unnoticed several minutes before, stood in the shadows watching and waiting. He had hopes that Mr. Mavrich would be able to talk a little sense into his troublesome patient.

At last Mr. Ledford muttered, "You'd never lie in bed an' let your ranch be run by a bunch of young whipper-snappers."

Norman smiled. "Don't forget I was laid up for weeks this fall, and my wife and Doc wouldn't let me do a thing. And," he added, "I was only a year or so older than Elbert is now when I took over the Triple Creek."

Turning his head restlessly, Mr. Ledford muttered and growled some things to himself and then in louder tones said, "Don't you have work to do, Elbert?"

"Yes, sir."

"Then get on with it and take Mavrich with you. He should've been a lawyer," the sick man grumbled before closing his eyes.

Mrs. Ledford was waiting in the hallway for them as Mr. Mavrich and Elbert descended the stairs. "I think it will be all right now, Mother," Elbert told her quietly, glancing back up the stairs. "I don't know if I can run a ranch and make it pay, but I'll sure try." He sighed and squared his shoulders. "You take care of Pa, Mother, and I'll take care of the ranch."

Mrs. Ledford nodded and, after kissing her son, slipped up the stairs leaving the two men to continue their way outside.

Neither one spoke until they had crossed the yard and were nearing the barn. "What do you think I should do first, Mr. Mavrich?"

Norman glanced about the yard. "Well, let's take a walk about the yards and see what will need done in the next few months."

"Remember, those papers are due by the end of the week," Miss Hearter reminded her class. As heads nodded, she smiled. "All right, class is dismissed."

There was a general clamor and clatter as the children snatched books and slates and raced for the door. "Charity," Orlena said, "can't you come home with me today?"

Turning to her friend, Charity shook her head. "I wish I could, I'd love to come see Beautiful Dreamer, but Mother needs me today. Perhaps I can come tomorrow."

Just then someone pushed between the girls and tried to squeeze past them.

Orlena stepped aside and then, noticing who the newcomer was, said eagerly, "Elvira, do you want to come home with me today and see the new foal?"

Picking up her lunch pail and not turning around, Elvira replied in a strained voice, "I can't. Mother expects me home right after school."

"Well, ask her if you can come tomorrow," Orlena begged, eager to show the new little horse to anyone.

Elvira's answer was noncommittal and she slowly moved away. Once she was out of earshot, Charity whispered, "She talked to you, Orlena, and I think she really wants to come. Why don't we pray that she'll really ask and then come?"

Orlena nodded and then bidding her friend good bye, skipped off down the street to the livery stable.

As Mr. Randolph was saddling Anything, Orlena told him about the new foal. She had hardly ever said much to the livery man, but her delight in naming the animal seemed to have taken away all her reserve that day.

Scratching his head as he looked after Orlena Mavrich as she rode away, Randolph muttered, "Well, she sure enough is different than when she first came."

As Orlena slid down from Anything before the barn, Lloyd appeared. "Where's Charity?" he asked, glancing around.

"She couldn't come," Orlena sighed dismally. "And I so wanted to show Beautiful Dreamer to her."

"Who?" Lloyd had taken Anything's reins and was leading the horse into the barn.

But Orlena didn't answer. She had hurried over to Lady's stall and was standing on tiptoe to see inside. "Hello, Lady. How's Beautiful Dreamer doing? There you are, you pretty little thing."

"Oh, did you name Lady's filly?" Lloyd asked as he unsaddled Anything and brushed her down.

"Uh huh. Oh!" Her cry caused Lloyd's head to turn quickly.

"What is it?"

"She's . . . she's, why, she's standing up! Beautiful Dreamer stood up! Lloyd, she did. She did! Come see!"

Lloyd was slightly amused at Orlena's excitement. Having been around horses all his life, it was difficult for him to imagine just what it must be like to see such a young creature standing for the first time. With a brush in one hand, he crossed the barn, tipped a bucket upside-down and said, "There, stand on that. You'll be able to see better."

Orlena wasted no time in mounting the bucket and leaned over the top of the half door, gazing in awe at the small foal nuzzling her mother's side for her supper. "Beautiful Dreamer," she mused half aloud. "The name fits you. Don't you think so, Lloyd?"

Lloyd had returned to Anything and, after letting her into her stall, asked, "What was that?"

Orlena repeated her question.

"Sure. Where'd you come up with the name anyway?"

Resting her chin on top of her folded arms, she replied, "It's the name of a song I heard once with Grandmother. I don't remember how it all goes though."

"Well, maybe Alden knows it and can play it on his fiddle." When he received no answer, Lloyd left the barn and strode to the house to see if Mrs. Mavrich had any work for him to do.

Supper was just about ready when Norman and Burns rode in and dismounted. Jenelle waited on the porch until Captain had been attended to and her husband had started for the house. Then she hurried to meet him.

"Hello, Darling," Norman greeted his wife affectionately. "How was your day?"

"Quiet. What about yours?"

Norman nodded and held open the kitchen door for Jenelle to pass in before him. "It was good, but I'm mighty hungry and something smells tasty."

Turning from the stove, Mrs. O'Connor smiled. "You're just in time to wash up and sit down, Norman, if you hurry," she told him briskly.

"Then I'd better do it," Norman laughed. "I won't be a minute, Jenelle."

CHAPTER 6

"I CAN'T LET GO!"

Once the family and Mrs. O'Connor were seated at the table and the meal had begun, Norman glanced over at his sister and asked, "Did you and Charity enjoy the afternoon?"

Spreading butter on her bread, Orlena replied, "Charity couldn't come today. But she is going to see if she can come tomorrow and . . ." she hesitated a moment.

"And what?" Norman prompted, curious.

"And I invited Elvira to come too."

"Did she accept?"

"I don't know." Orlena bit into her slice of bread thoughtfully.

"You mean she talked to you and didn't refuse the invitation?" Jenelle asked.

Orlena nodded.

"Well," Jenelle looked pleased. "I would say it was a step in the right direction, even if she doesn't end up coming tomorrow. But, Orlena, if she and Charity do come tomorrow, how are they going to get home again?"

"Elvira walks home from school like I do." Orlena looked puzzled.

"Dear, that's in the middle of the afternoon. The Bar X is on the other side of Rough Rock. It would take twice as long for her to get home from here as it does from school."

Orlena's shoulders slumped and her face, which had

been so bright, sobered.

On seeing that, Jenelle turned to her husband, "Norman, could someone take the girls home tomorrow if they come?"

Slowly drumming his fingers on the table, Norman sat silent a few minutes. Then he sighed and began to shake his head. "I don't see how—" he began. "I can't spare any men tomorrow and I already promised Elbert I'd ride out to look at a new pasture tomorrow morning, and by the time I get back . . . I'm sorry, Orlena."

Mrs. O'Connor, who had been quietly eating her supper as the conversation went on around her, looked up and said, "Perhaps Elbert would be willing to ride back with you and pick up his sister and see to it that Charity gets safely home."

At this suggestion, Orlena clapped her hands. "Oh, Mrs. O'Connor!" she exclaimed, "that is a wonderful idea!"

"Do you think Elbert would mind?" Jenelle asked Norman.

After glancing first at his sister and then at his wife, he replied, "I don't think he would this once."

"Oh, if they can only come!"

There was a pleasant fire in the fireplace, for even though the days were warm and sunny, the evenings, after the sun had set, were still rather cool. For several minutes Norman had been sitting idle, staring into the flames with a frown now and then crossing his face. Mrs. O'Connor and Orlena had gone up to bed some time before, but Jenelle had decided to wait for Norman to be ready. The clock struck the half hour and still he remained motionless. At last, unable to stand the quiet any longer, Jenelle said softly, "Norman, what is bothering you?"

"Huh?" Norman looked up, startled. "What was that, Jenelle?"

"I asked what was bothering you. You've been staring at the fire for thirty minutes without saying a word."

Sighing, Norman uncrossed and straightened his legs. "Sorry, I guess I was doing some thinking."

"What about?"

For a moment Norman hesitated as though trying to collect his thoughts, then he said, "I guess I was wondering if the advice I gave Elbert was good." When Jenelle looked inquiringly at him, he continued. "I told him to stop second guessing himself. He's got to start standing by his decisions unless he has good reasons for changing them. He'll tell the men to start riding fence on the north line, but then he wonders if the south line might be down and changes his orders." He gave another sigh. "Perhaps I should have waited until he had a little more experience before telling him that."

"Now who's second guessing themselves?" Jenelle chided with a little laugh.

"Huh?" For a moment Norman's face was blank and then a grin began to creep over it and he laughed. "You're right. I reckon I ought to stop second guessing myself if I'm going to hand out the same advice." He yawned. "What do you say to heading up to bed?"

To her delight, Charity was allowed to go to the Triple Creek Ranch after school. Both Charity and Orlena tried to persuade Elvira to join them, but she tossed her head and said it wouldn't be worth her time and started off alone for the Bar X.

"I did want her to come," Orlena sighed.

"I know, but why don't you invite Flo and Jenny. They live near the Triple Creek," Charity suggested.

This thought pleased Orlena so much that before she knew it, Flo and Jenny Carmond, and a few other children whose ranches were out that way, had been asked to joined them. All were eager to see the first spring foal and set off at once.

Thus it was that Mrs. O'Connor, glancing out the window, suddenly gave an exclamation of surprise.

"What is it, Mrs. O'Connor?" Jenelle wondered,

looking up from her knitting.

"Tis a group of children all coming down the lane, indeed, and sure it's Orlena herself leading the way!"

The two women stood by the window and watched as the children, after dumping their books on the wagon bed, hurried into the barn. "If they're looking for Lady and her filly," Jenelle remarked, "they'll have to check the pasture, for I heard Norman tell Scott to let them out so Lady could graze today. Perhaps I should go tell them—"

Just then the children came out of the barn and began looking around until a shout from one of the boys brought the rest running to the pasture fence.

"I don't think I need to tell them after all," Jenelle smiled. She sank back into her chair. "If they need anything, they'll come to the house."

When at last the other children left for their own ranches, Orlena and Charity slowly made their way to the house talking. Entering the kitchen, Charity smiled. "Hello, Mrs. Mavrich, Mrs. O'Connor."

"Hello, Charity," Jenelle returned the smile. "Didn't Elvira come with you girls?"

Orlena shook her head. "She wouldn't. She said it wasn't worth her time and then went home."

"You'll just have to keep praying for her and trying to be kind. Things are difficult and strange at her house right now with her father sick, and I'm sure both her brothers are thinking about the ranch and Mrs. Ledford probably doesn't have much time for her right now."

Charity sat down on one of the kitchen chairs and set her books on the table. "I feel sorry for her, Mrs. Mavrich."

Jenelle nodded and smiled sympathetically. Then, seeing the sober looks on the girls' faces, changed the subject. "Have you girls looked for the new kittens yet?"

"Kittens!" Charity exclaimed, "Oh, Mrs. Mavrich, are there really kittens?"

"That's what Scott said this morning. He saw the mother moving one of them in the barn. I believe he said it looked about a week old."

"Oh, let's go find them, Orlena!" Charity was eager.

Hesitating a moment, Orlena hung back. She still hadn't learned to like the barn cats and she wasn't sure she wanted to find a nest of them. "I don't think I should in my school dress," she began.

Jenelle eyed both girls a moment and then said quickly, "Both of you run up and change. Charity, I think one of Orlena's dresses will fit you so you won't get yours torn or dirty. Run along now, both of you."

They departed, Orlena thankful for an excuse to put off searching for the kittens and Charity eager to discover the hidden nest.

Listening to their footsteps fade on the stairs, Jenelle sighed and dropped her knitting. "If I weren't so tired, I'd like nothing better than to go search for that nest myself."

"Humph," snorted Mrs. O'Connor. "A fine thing it would be indeed for you to be climbing around the barn in your condition. And what would Norman be saying to you if he were to find out?" Setting a pan of water on the table, Mrs. O'Connor settled herself on a chair and began peeling potatoes.

"Let me help with those," Jenelle begged, setting her knitting in her basket. "I'm feeling so useless, I have to do something or . . . or . . . or I will go and hunt for those kittens!" she finished with more energy than she felt.

With a little smile, Mrs. O'Connor handed a knife to Mrs. Mavrich, and soon the potato peels were flying.

The quick sound of steps in the next room sounded before the two girls returned to the kitchen. "Come on, Orlena," Charity was saying, pulling on her friend's hand, "if you think Beautiful Dreamer is sweet, wait until you see the kittens!"

"Perhaps I should help with supper," Orlena offered, but her sister waved her away.

"Go on. I want to know how many kittens there are."

Still reluctant, Orlena allowed herself to be pulled from

the house and out to the barn. There she looked around. Where were they supposed to look for a nest of kittens? "Charity, how are we ever going to find them?" she asked.

"We look. Come on into the loft. That's where most cats have their nests because it's out of the way." Charity was already half-way up the ladder.

Watching Charity climb the ladder, Orlena looked nervous. She had never been in the loft before and couldn't remember ever climbing a ladder either. But she didn't want Charity to think she was afraid, so she followed her.

For over thirty minutes the girls searched the loft and found nothing. At last Charity dropped down onto the hay and whispered, "Let's just sit here and listen and watch. Maybe Mrs. Cat will come or maybe we'll hear the kittens."

Orlena was glad to sit down and rest. She felt warm and tired. "Charity," she whispered, after several minutes of silence. "Do you think Elvira will be at the Sunday School picnic on Saturday?"

"I don't know. She doesn't always come to Sunday School, you know. But Elbert comes to church, maybe he'll bring her."

"I hope so."

They fell silent again and then a faint rustling was heard in the hay behind them. Quietly the girls turned their heads. A small movement caught Charity's eye and she motioned towards it. Orlena nodded and as softly as they could they crept towards it. Lifting a leaning board, Charity suddenly breathed, "Orlena!"

Ducking her head under Charity's arm, Orlena gasped. There in a warm nest deep in the hay were the kittens. Five little furry balls, two orange, one grey, one black and one white and black.

"Oh!" That one word seemed to be the only thing Orlena could say as she gazed at the small creatures.

Charity nodded. "I didn't think there would be five," she whispered. "I just wish they were a little older so we could hold them."

"Can't we hold them now?" Orlena whispered back.

"We could, but if we do, Mrs. Cat would probably move them and then we'd have to hunt for them all over again." Looking around, Charity gently leaned the board back in place and motioned to Orlena. "I think if we were to climb up and sit on those rafters, we could watch the nest and see if Mrs. Cat moves them."

Orlena looked up and shook her head, her eyes wide.

"Come on," Charity begged. "It isn't very high up and if we did fall we would only land in the hay. Please!"

"I . . . I've never climbed anything like that in my life," Orlena began, "I don't think—"

"Don't start thinking now. I'll show you how."

Still staring at the broad rafter beams above, Orlena swallowed hard. "Are they safe?"

"Of course they are," Charity assured. "Watch." In less time than it takes to tell about it, Charity had clambered up a sloping board, grasped hold of the rafter and swung herself up. "See," she smiled down at Orlena's amazed and slightly frightened face, "There's nothing to it. Come on."

It took several minutes of coaxing before Orlena slowly inched her way across the loft over to the board. And it was only with Charity's step-by-step instructions that Orlena finally managed to climb up onto the rafter.

"Scoot over this way some more," Charity motioned. "It's mighty uncomfortable to sit bent so far over where the roof slopes. Out here you can sit up, and," she added seeing her friend hesitate, "there's a joist here you can hang on to if you want."

It took Orlena almost as long to scoot across that rafter as it had taken her to climb up in the first place. When at last she reached Charity's side and had a firm hold of the joist, she gave a long sigh. "I don't think I'll be getting down any time soon."

Charity laughed and then pointed down below them. From their vantage point the girls could look down and see the kittens in the nest. "Now we just have to wait for Mrs.

Cat to come take care of her babies," she whispered.

For several minutes the girls sat, Orlena tense and rigid, Charity at ease and with swinging feet. At last Orlena said softly, "Charity, how did you learn to climb so well?"

Charity gave a giggle. "Well, Katie and I used to tag along after Lloyd when we were small, and he taught us to climb trees and anything else he climbed so we wouldn't be left behind. Poor Mother wasn't ever sure where she'd find us because it wasn't long before we could climb as well as Lloyd. I admit it isn't very ladylike to climb trees in town, now that I'm almost thirteen, so I rarely get a chance to climb anything."

Silence once again descended on the two girls in the rafters until Charity suddenly nudged Orlena and pointed. There below them was one of the barn cats. She approached the nest and looked around. The girls watched in delight when she jumped into the nest and began washing the kittens vigorously with her tongue before settling down so they could eat. So absorbed were the girls in the doings in the nest that neither of them realized just how dark the barn was growing.

The sudden sound of booted feet on the hard floor below the ladder, caused Mrs. Cat to abandon her babies and disappear into a dark corner. Charity turned her head towards the ladder. "Lloyd!" she exclaimed in delight.

The young hand glanced quickly about the loft.

"Up here," Charity called, waving her hand.

Lloyd looked up. "What—" he began. "Charity Hearter, what in thunder are you doing up there?" he demanded, striding over to stand under the two girls and look up at them.

"We were watching the kittens. Their nest is just behind you under that board."

Lloyd didn't even turn around. "You two had better come down and get a move on into the house before Mrs. Mavrich comes out looking for you. There's a storm blowing in, and it's moving fast." He held up his arms and his sister jumped lightly into them.

"When will I get home? Mother will worry if there's a storm coming."

"We wouldn't make it before the storm hit," he told her. Then he turned back to Orlena who was still sitting on the rafter. "All right, Orlena, jump."

"I . . . I . . ." her breathing was quick and her face frightened. "I can't!"

"Yes, you can," Charity replied. "I did. Lloyd won't let you fall. Come on."

Orlena shook her head. They didn't understand. "I . . . I can't!" There were tears in her voice. "I can't let go."

"Shall I go up and try to help her?" Charity asked.

But her brother shook his head. "Not yet. Orlena, close your eyes and pretend you are sitting on the kitchen table."

Squeezing her eyes shut, Orlena remained still for a few seconds and then her eyes flew wide open. "They won't stay closed," she whimpered.

"Then scoot back the way you came up," Lloyd instructed. "I'll stand below to catch you if you slip."

But Orlena remained where she was. "I can't let go," she wailed.

CHAPTER 7

THE SUNDAY SCHOOL PICNIC

Just then a shout sounded from below. "Hearter?"

"Scott, come up and give me a hand," Lloyd called back and in another minute the ranch wrangler appeared at the top of the ladder.

"What's going on?" he asked, catching sight of Charity and Lloyd and then raising his eyes to the silent form of Orlena. A slight smile twitched the corners of his mouth. "How's she stuck?"

"Fear. Can you get her unstuck so they can get to the house before the storm hits or Mrs. Mavrich comes out looking for them?"

"Sure thing." And before Orlena quite realized it, Scott had swung himself up and was straddling the rafter beside her. "Now what seems to be the trouble," he asked easily, eyeing her.

"I can't get down," she whimpered. "I can't jump and I can't move because I can't let go."

Scott could see the death grip she had on the rafter and brace. Reaching into his pocket he pulled out his bandana. After tying a loop in one end of it he reached around the frightened girl and held the loop close to her hand. "Here we are. Just grab a hold of this," he coaxed. "Don't worry, it's plenty safe."

With a shaking hand, but feeling a little more secure

with a strong arm on either side of her, Orlena somehow managed to shift her hold to the loop in the bandana.

"That's right," Scott said softly to her. "See, this isn't so hard after all." Then calling down to Lloyd, he said, "Make a loop in your bandana and toss it up, Hearter."

"What is he going to do with those?" Charity asked, watching her brother swiftly tie his bandana and pass it up to Scott.

Lloyd grinned. "Watch and see."

It took a little longer to coax Orlena's other hand to change its grip of the solid rafter to the seemingly flimsy loop of the bandana, but Scott hadn't sweet talked and coaxed horses for several years for nothing. As soon as both loops were gripped securely, he said, "Now, take a deep breath and relax."

Orlena tried and the next moment felt herself falling, and then a pair of strong hands caught her, and she was set on her feet. For a moment she could only stand staring, not quite sure of what had just happened.

Charity laughed and hugged her. "You did it, Orlena! You jumped."

Orlena shook her head and looked at the bandanas still in her hands. "No, I was pushed."

Scott and Lloyd laughed. "Either way, it got you down. Now you two had better skedaddle for the house before the rain lets loose."

Relinquishing the bandanas with still somewhat shaky hands, Orlena whispered, "Thank you," and hurried after her friend.

Jenelle was looking anxiously towards the barn as the girls raced for the house. When they arrived on the porch, she gave a sigh of relief. "I was starting to worry about you two. Let's get in out of this wind."

Pushing the girls into the kitchen before her, Jenelle took one more look up the lane, her face wearing a slightly worried expression.

"Mrs. O'Connor," Charity exclaimed, pushing back her

light, wind-blown hair from her face, "we found the kittens!"

"There are five of them," Orlena added. "But I got stuck on the rafter and Scott had to push me off and where's Norman? How is Charity going to get home with the storm? Lloyd said they couldn't make it before it hit, but Mrs. Hearter is going to be worried."

Jenelle looked bewildered as she turned from the window. "Orlena, one question at a time and one subject at a time, please. There are the rest of the hands and Hardrich, but where is Norman?"

"Stop fretting, Jenelle," Mrs. O'Connor chided gently. "'Tis not a bit a rain or wind that will be harmin' him entirely." She turned to the girls. "Best get yourselves washed up sure, for the supper is nearly ready and the table isn't set."

Moments later Orlena and Charity had the table set and were helping Mrs. O'Connor carry the dishes out to the dining room while Jenelle kept her place at the window and watched as the rain began to fall.

Leaning her head wearily against the cool window pane, Jenelle closed her eyes a moment and sent up a silent prayer for her husband's safety. When she opened her eyes, she gave an exclamation and started to the door. "Oh, it's Norman! Thank God, he's home!"

"Jenelle!" Orlena called, running to her sister's side. "You can't go out in that. Why it's pouring!"

"I'm not going farther than the porch," Jenelle assured, her hand on the door latch.

Before Orlena could protest further, the sound of a quick tread was heard, the door was opened and Norman entered the kitchen.

"Whew!" he gasped. "It's wet outside! Darling, you weren't going out there, were you?" he asked, turning to Jenelle who was about to fling her arms around him. "Whoa, wait a minute," and Norman quickly held back his wife. "Let me get my jacket off; I don't want you as wet as I am."

"I wouldn't care," Jenelle smiled.

"Well, I would." As soon as his hat and jacket were off,

he tenderly kissed her. Then looking up, he caught sight of Charity's sober face in the doorway. "Charity, you are spending the night here. No one is going anywhere tonight with this storm."

Charity bit her lip and then whispered, "Mother will be worried sick if I don't get home."

Sitting down to pull off his boots, Norman replied, "No, she won't. I stopped by your house on my way home. I knew a storm was coming and thought it best if you just remained here for the night. You can go in to school with Orlena in the morning."

Orlena gave a gasp. "Spending the night? Here? Charity!" She rushed to her friend and seized her hands. "We can talk all night and—"

"No, you can't," Norman interrupted. "And you both have homework to do. Now, Jenelle, if you'll excuse me for a few minutes, I think I'll put on some dry clothes before I sit down to eat."

Supper that evening was not a quiet affair, for Orlena, who was bubbling over with excitement at the prospect of having a guest for the night, chattered on. When at last, having told all about the children coming to see Beautiful Dreamer, the kittens and the experience on the rafter, she began to eat, Norman told about his day at the Bar X. "Edgar was hitching up the buggy to fetch Elvira home from here," he remarked, "as Elbert went to tell his mother where he was heading. A few minutes later he came and told me Elvira had come straight home from school. Well, I started for home and, on seeing how quickly the storm was moving in, decided to stop at the Hearter's. Everything was fine there, Charity, so you needn't worry." Mr. Mavrich flashed a smiled at their young guest.

"Norman," Orlena asked, pausing as she began to help clear the dishes away, "if Elvira had come and her brother had ridden here to take her back, would they have been stuck here too because of the storm?"

"Probably. Why?"

She shook her head. "I just thought of it and wondered." Turning away with a stack of plates in her hands she remarked, "It sure is raining. Will we be able to get to school tomorrow?"

"You should if the creeks don't rise," her brother answered. "Now you'd better get those dishes taken care of so you girls can get your homework done."

Orlena groaned.

The creeks had risen during the night, but not high enough to prevent Norman from taking the girls to school in the buggy the following morning, and by afternoon the sun had dried many of the puddles in the road.

₵

Orlena gazed eagerly around at the folks mingling and visiting about the green meadow and under the budding shade trees behind the manse. It had finally arrived: the Sunday School picnic! Mrs. O'Connor and Jenelle had fried chicken and baked pies, and some of the hands from the Triple Creek Ranch were there. Jenelle had told her there would be games and food and music and singing. Orlena had never attended anything like a Sunday School picnic before and she had looked forward with great anticipation to the day.

Her thoughts were interrupted by her brother's voice. "Orlena, do you care to join us?"

Turning her head quickly, Orlena realized that Norman had already assisted Jenelle and Mrs. O'Connor down from the carriage and he was waiting for her. She allowed him to lift her down and then took the blanket he handed her, though her eyes still roved about searching.

"Are you looking for someone?" A voice spoke behind her.

"Charity!" Orlena whirled around to see her friend's bright face.

"Good morning, Charity," Jenelle smiled. "Where is the rest of your family? Was your mother able to make it?"

"Good morning, Mrs. Mavrich. Yes, Mother is here. She is hoping you'll spread your blanket near us and join us for lunch. And I think Lloyd hopes so too," she laughed. "He hasn't stopped talking about all the food you prepared and the pies you baked."

Jenelle's merry laugh rippled on the air and she turned to Norman who had taken a large hamper from the back of the carriage. "Let's join the Hearters, Norman. It would be a shame if Lloyd couldn't enjoy some of the fried chicken and pies we brought."

Norman also laughed and agreed at once. Charity led the way and soon the Mavriches were established beside Mrs. Hearter. The girls were dismissed, and hand in hand they disappeared into the crowd and weren't seen again until their hunger drove them back in time for dinner.

"Jenelle," Norman asked, having finished off his first piece of fried chicken, "did you or Mrs. O'Connor fry this chicken?"

"Why, what's wrong with it?" Jenelle asked anxiously.

"Nothing. I just remembered you had asked me whose fried chicken I liked better and I don't think I ever told you."

Jenelle looked puzzled. "Didn't you say you liked Mrs. O'Connor's better? I thought you . . ." she hesitated, confused.

Norman laughed. "Whichever one I'm eating at the time is my favorite, so I think I'll have another piece."

A general laugh went around the group of friends and the rest of the meal was eaten with great enjoyment.

Later that afternoon, as Orlena and Charity were strolling about the grounds and wondering why Elvira Ledford hadn't come with her mother and brother Edgar, they heard someone calling them. Turning, they saw Jonah Hughes hurrying over to them.

"Todd Alden has his fiddle out," he panted. "Some of us are going to see if he'll tell us about his rattlesnake tail."

"What rattlesnake tail?" Orlena asked. "I never knew he had one?"

Jonah looked astonished. "He's never told you one of his tall tales about that tail?" When Orlena shook her head, he looked at Charity and then back at Orlena. "Then come on!"

As they hurried over to the wagons, Jonah explained. "You see, Alden's got this fiddle that was his grandfather's and inside it is a rattlesnake tail. We've all often wondered why it's in there and why he keeps it there, and every time we ask him he has a different story."

"We never know what is going to happen," Charity put in. "There he is." She pointed to a wagon where a group was beginning to gather, mostly children, but many grown folks were also interested in "Alden's tall tales" as people around called his stories.

When the three children arrived and pushed their way near the front, they could see Alden sitting on the back of the wagon, his legs swinging slightly as he tuned his old fiddle.

"Mr. Alden," a young boy called out, "how'd that rattlesnake tail get inside that fiddle?"

After drawing his bow a few times across the strings, Alden pushed his hat back and rested his instrument on his knee. "Well now," he began, "that's a story of a long time ago."

The children sat down on the grass and prepared to listen, Orlena among them.

CHAPTER 8

FIDDLIN' AROUND WITH A RATTLESNAKE

"Way back when my grandfather was a young man, he'd take on some odd jobs here and there playing his fiddle for a barn raisin', or a shin-dig of sorts, as a way to earn a bit more money. You see, he was planning on being married come the fall and, well, you folks know how it is about getting' married.

"Well, this particular day, Grandpa was riding his horse . . ." He paused and scratched his chin. "Now what was that horse's name?"

"Lightning," someone suggested.

Nodding quickly, Alden said, "That was it. He was riding his horse, Lightning, and suddenly that horse went lame on him. Grandpa climbed down and, what do you know, that horse had pulled a tendon.

"So there Grandpa was, out in the vast range with a lame horse and a shin-dig to get to. My grandfather was a quick thinking man, and he decided he could walk and lead his horse, so off they started.

"Now they hadn't gotten very far when they heard a sound that strikes fear into most critters. It was the ominous sound of a rattler's tail. Lightning, being a horse and not knowing where that snake was, reared up quite sudden and almost pulled Grandpa off his feet. Somehow Grandpa managed to hang on to the reins, but the case with his fiddle in it, went sailing off the horse's back. Now Grandpa was a man of quick thinking, as I may have mentioned before, and he tried to pull his gun because he knew if he shot the snake, the horse would calm down. The only trouble was, Lightning wouldn't stand still long enough for Grandpa to get his gun out. Grandpa wasn't ever what you might call a fast gun." Alden paused in his story and looked around at the wide eyes of the children and the amused looks of the older members of his audience.

"Grandpa was just about to give up and let his horse run away, when Lightning just settled down as calm as could be. Grandpa listened but he couldn't hear the sound of that rattler any more. 'That's odd, I wonder what happened to that snake?' he said to himself. There wasn't anyone else to say it to except his horse. Well, folks, he didn't have time to stand and wonder about the peculiar habits of snakes, he had a shin-dig to get to. Looking around he saw his fiddle case lying some feet away and strode over to fetch it.

Alden leaned forward and his voice dropped. "As he bent down to pick up the case, he saw it was sitting right smack down on that old rattler's head. Yes, sir! See, when that case flew through the air, it landed on the snake and, wouldn't you know, killed it right straight off. Now my grandpa, he looked at that snake and says he, 'I declare that snake's got somethin' that don't belong to him any more.' And he cut off the tail. Then, opening the case, just to make sure the fiddle wasn't hurt, he dropped the tail inside, and off he set for the shin-dig with his fiddle under his arm and his horse trailing behind."

"But how'd the tail get in the fiddle?" Jonah called.

"Well, Grandpa thought, since that fiddle had done such a good job of killing the snake, it ought to have the tail, so he dropped it inside an' it's been there ever since."

Orlena applauded with rest of the crowd, but asked, as she and Charity were walking away with Jonah, "Are all the stories like that one?"

"Oh, no," Jonah assured. "That was one of the most interesting ones. But I've got to get to the race, See you later!" And he dashed away.

Both girls were quiet for several minutes and then Charity asked, looked at Orlena, "What are you thinking about?"

"I was just wondering why Elvira didn't come."

"Let's go ask Mrs. Ledford. She's right over there." Charity pointed to a few ladies who were watching the boys' race.

Orlena nodded. She did want to know if Elvira was sick.

"Excuse me, Mrs. Ledford?" Charity said sweetly.

The woman turned. "Yes? Oh, good afternoon, Charity, Orlena. What can I do for you?"

"We were just wondering where Elvira was?"

"Is she sick?" Orlena asked.

Mrs. Ledford shook her head with a smile. "No, she's not sick. The sweet girl just insisted that I needed to get away from the ranch for a little while and said that she would take care of her pa. I'll admit to you that I wasn't sure I could enjoy the day, but I do believe the change has been good for me. Is there any message you want me to take to Elvira?"

"Please tell her we missed her," Charity replied. "And that we hope to see her in Sunday School tomorrow."

"Thank you, Dears. I'll be sure to tell her. And I think her oldest brother will be happy to bring her to church and Sunday School in the morning."

The girls said good bye and slipped away.

"Do you really think she'll come tomorrow?" Orlena asked, when they were out of earshot of Mrs. Ledford.

Charity shrugged. "We'll just have to wait and see."

Strolling along, the girls soon rejoined Mrs. Hearter and Jenelle back under the shade tree where they had been enjoying the music and visiting with those who came by to chat.

"There you are, Girls," Mrs. Hearter greeted them. "The singing is going to begin shortly. Connie just stopped by to tell us."

Jenelle gave a sigh and shifted her position against the tree. "I know I'll enjoy the singing, but I'll be thankful when the evening is over."

"Are you feeling all right?" Mrs. Hearter asked anxiously.

"Just a little tired," Jenelle admitted, smiling. "But don't tell Norman, I wouldn't want him to worry."

Orlena looked around. "Where is Mrs. O'Connor?"

"Mrs. Kirby took her off to introduce her to a few people she hadn't met before," answered Jenelle with another sigh. "Orlena, would you mind fetching me a glass of water, please?"

Orlena rose at once and hurried to the manse. She was soon back with the water and Jenelle smiled gratefully. A bell rang announcing the time for singing and Norman and Lloyd were seen moments later hurrying over to the waiting ladies.

"Sorry to be late, Darling," Norman apologized, as he reached for her hand to help her up. "Lloyd was beating me in a second round of horse shoes."

"He's been good at that game since he was little," Mrs. Hearter remarked, smiling up at her tall son as she leaned on his arm. "His father taught him to play it almost as soon as he taught him to ride a horse."

Norman chuckled. "No wonder he's good. Where's Mrs. O'Connor?"

Jenelle explained and then added, "I'm sure she'll find us." Jenelle was right; before many songs had been sung, the older woman rejoined the Mavriches. The singing was an informal affair, much enjoyed by the ranchers and town folk alike. Anyone who could play a fiddle or harmonica was invited to join, and folks could sing or just sit and listen to the music as the evening slowly drew on and the sun began sinking in the western sky.

Suddenly, in the quiet between songs, came the thunder of galloping hooves and as every head turned, a rider dashed into the yard and reined up sharply. "Mr. Mavrich! Sheriff!"

"That's Tracy!" Norman exclaimed, hurriedly pushing his way through the crowd. "What's happened?" he demanded as soon as he was close to the rider.

"Rustlers, sir. St. John and Hardrich exchanged some shots with them and they rode off, but they didn't go far."

"What do you mean? How do you know?" Sheriff Hughes had by this time reached the excited young man.

"Davis claimed he could still see them back on the far ridge near Penny Creek."

Alden, Scott, Burns and Hearter, the Triple Creek hands who had attended the picnic, exchanged glances. "Davis couldn't see that far, Matt," Burns scoffed.

Drawing a deep breath, Tracy explained quickly. "He was riding Shad out on the range and heard the shots. He was about to ride in when he saw some mounted men racing by near the south fence. He followed them a few miles until they seemed to slow at the ridge, then he came back and told Hardrich. Hardrich sent me out to find you, sir."

"Was anyone hurt by the shots?"

Tracy shook his head. "No, sir."

"Want me to saddle up the horses, Mr. Mavrich?" Scott asked.

Norman didn't reply right away.

"And shall I get the carriage hitched up?" Lloyd questioned.

The ranchers had gathered around and were talking in low tones together, waiting to see if they were wanted and what Norman Mavrich would do. For half a minute Norman stood deep in thought. Then he spoke. "Scott, Burns, Alden, saddle up and be ready to ride. Hearter, you have to see your mother and sisters home—"

"We can see to that, Mavrich," one of the townsmen assured quickly. "Don't worry about them."

"I don't want to take the women back to the ranch . . ." Norman frowned thoughtfully.

Reverend Kirby stepped up and placed a hand on Norman's arm. "Let your wife, sister and Mrs. O'Connor stay with us. There is plenty of room in the manse."

"Thank you, Reverend. That would help." He turned quickly to his youngest hand who was waiting with impatience for orders. "Hearter, tell your mother where you're going then saddle Spitfire and be ready to ride. Sheriff, are you coming? Good." He glanced around. "I need a horse."

"Well I can get you one from the livery, Mavrich," Randolph promised and then hurried away at Norman's nod.

"Mavrich," Mr. Bates called out from the crowd, "you want more help to catch them rustlers?"

Looking up suddenly from his fixed stare at nothing, he became aware of the conversation around him. After glancing quickly around at the men gathered near him, he called sharply, "Barker, Wilson, Maynard." As three young men pushed their way forward, Mr. Mavrich asked, "You three still wanting to work for me?"

"Yes, sir!" The answers came as one.

"You're hired. Get your horses and things and be in front of the sheriff's office in ten minutes. Tracy, dismount and give Apache a drink and cool him off a little." He slapped the horse's neck gently as he added, "We ride back in ten minutes." When Norman Mavrich gave an order to his men, he expected instant obedience and rarely waited to see his instructions followed out before turning to someone or something else. Turning from the horse and rider, Mavrich began to push his way through the crowd, answering questions as he went. "No, Bates, I don't think I'll need you tonight. Thanks. Best you all keep an eye on your own ranches. . . . No, the Triple Creek will have a dozen men tonight. . . . I doubt the rustlers will stick around waiting for us."

As he at last reached the place where he had left his wife, sister and housekeeper, Norman heard Jenelle speaking.

"Mrs. O'Connor, we'd better get things packed up now. Norman is going to want to get back to the ranch and we don't want to delay him."

"Hold on a minute," Norman ordered quickly. "The things can be packed up later." As his wife turned to him, her eyes wide with unasked questions, he paused to kiss her before saying, "You, Orlena and Mrs. O'Connor are going to be staying here at the manse tonight, Sweetheart."

"But—"

Norman's arm was around her and a tender pressure of his hand silenced her. "The men and I are riding back with the sheriff in ten minutes. I don't want to have you three at the ranch house alone to worry about now. Reverend Kirby invited you to remain here, and I'll feel more at ease because I'll know you are safe."

Lifting tear-filled eyes and a brave smile to the serious and somewhat concerned face above her, Jenelle whispered, "Promise me you'll be careful."

"I promise, Darling. And promise me that you'll try not to worry."

Jenelle nodded, afraid her voice would quiver if she should try to speak.

Before more could be said, Mrs. Kirby hurried quickly over. "Mr. Kirby just told me about it," she said. "Don't worry about your wife, Mr. Mavrich. Or your sister either. Mrs. O'Connor and I will see to it that they are well taken care of."

Norman had only time for a brief word of thanks to Mrs. Kirby, a quick but clinging kiss for his wife, and he was gone, hurrying away with his quick stride towards the livery to get his horse before meeting the men.

Orlena watched him go with a bewildered expression. Things had happened so quickly that she wasn't sure what was going on. "Jenelle," she asked, "why is Norman leaving us here?"

Giving a tired sigh, Jenelle put an arm around her young sister's shoulders. "Cattle rustlers are working the Triple Creek tonight, and Norman is heading back with the hands to see if they can catch them."

"Working? Why would Norman hire cattle rustlers? I

thought they were men who stole cattle?"

With a little laugh, Jenelle attempted to explain. "Working the ranch simply means that they are trying to steal from the ranch."

"Oh."

CHAPTER 9

NEW DEPUTIES

Somehow the news of the attempted cattle stealing at the largest ranch in the area had put a damper on the end of the Sunday School picnic. Ranchers were eager to reach their own ranches before it was completely dark, and their wives quickly gathered picnic baskets and children, trying not to appear nervous. The boys of the ranches were full of excitement and bragged about what they would do if any thieving rustlers appeared when they were around. The town folk assisted in hitching up wagons, finding misplaced children, and offering help should any be needed in hunting down the bandits and bringing them to justice.

In all the confusion which followed the departure of her brother, Orlena didn't notice Mrs. O'Connor or Jenelle's disappearance. Feeling dazed by the sudden turn of events, she wandered over to a bench set in the middle of what would later be a blooming flower garden. There she sat, not really thinking, but watching the bustle and activity and trying to take in and understand what had happened in the last half an hour. When someone sat down beside her and a voice spoke, she started.

"The night air is starting to grow cool, Orlena. Won't you come in?" It was Reverend Kirby.

Glancing around, Orlena asked in surprise, "Is everyone gone?"

Reverend Kirby smiled. "Yes, and your sister was starting to grow anxious about you. Perhaps we should go inside now."

With a nod, Orlena stood up and brushed her dress off absentmindedly. "Do you think Norman will really be in danger, Mr. Kirby?"

"That is hard to say, Orlena. If the sheriff, Norman, and their men catch up with the ones stealing cattle, there could be a fight."

"With guns?"

"Yes. Are you worried about him?"

Orlena didn't answer right away but walked slowly beside the minister across the quiet grounds where only an hour before the sound of music and singing had filled the air. "I suppose I am. I mean, I should be, shouldn't I?" she looked up. "Everything was so sudden and I don't know what to think now. I don't want Norman to be in danger. Why couldn't he have been a lawyer instead of a rancher?" She sighed before answering her own question. "Because he'd hate the city. Maybe they won't catch the thieves. Surely they had plenty of time to ride away."

The minister didn't reply and Orlena looked up. "Is Mrs. O'Connor worried?"

With a smile Rev. Kirby replied, "Not that I could tell. And your sister is taking things calmly."

"Then I needn't worry." And Orlena smiled brightly and talked quite cheerfully the rest of the evening. But later, after the house was dark and still, stories she had read or heard of western bandits flooded her mind, and tears began chasing each other down her cheeks as she imagined her brother killed or in deadly peril.

"Orlena," a soft voice broke in upon her thoughts and Jenelle sat down on the bed beside her. "What is wrong?"

With a burst of sobs, Orlena buried her face in her pillow for a minute. Then, feeling her sister's calming touch, she lifted her head and sat up, choking back a sob. "I'm afraid! Jenelle, I'm afraid for Norman! What if he's badly hurt right now or even—"

Jenelle's hand was firmly placed over Orlena's mouth and she said almost sternly, "Stop that kind of talk, Orlena. It's not going to help anyone. You are letting your imagination get the better of you instead of trusting the Lord to take care of things."

Swallowing hard, Orlena blinked back her tears.

Jenelle's voice grew soft as she put an arm about the young girl so new to the dangers and hardships of ranch life and inexperienced in casting all her cares on the One who said He would bear them for her. "I want to tell you something, Orlena. Something that Mrs. O'Connor's mother used to tell her. It was the night of the stampede, and Mrs. O'Connor and I were waiting for Norman to come back to the house. We didn't know there was any stampede, but I knew there could be danger with such a storm and I was worrying. Mrs. O'Connor said that worrying is a sign that you should be praying. And you know, Orlena," Jenelle whispered, pulling her sister closer, "she was right."

Drawing a quivering breath, Orlena rested her head against Jenelle. "Can we pray for him now?"

"Of course." And slipping to their knees beside the bed, Jenelle and Orlena Mavrich took their worries to the Father. Orlena had never prayed aloud before someone else, and it was with hesitation that she began. But she soon forgot that other ears besides the loving Savior were listening.

When morning dawned at the Triple Creek Ranch, it found Norman Mavrich, the sheriff and a group of tired men unsaddling their horses at the barn. "Well," Mr. Mavrich remarked, lifting the saddle from Captain's broad back, "they gave us the slip that time, but we'll catch them yet. No one is going to rustle cattle around here and get away with it."

"I reckon not," Sheriff Hughes agreed. "And, Mavrich, I've been thinking. I'm going to deputize you and some of the other ranchers because I can't be in every place at the same time. This would also give you the authority you need should something happen on the ranch when you can't reach me."

Norman nodded. "All right, Sheriff, but I wish you'd deputize Hardrich too."

The sheriff nodded in approval. "I'll do that. Right now. Both of you raise your right hands." In another minute the sheriff shook hands with his new deputies and remarked, "Something tells me I'm going to wish I had you both as deputies around town all the time, after this business is over with."

Mr. Mavrich raised an eyebrow. "Sorry, Sheriff, I'm sticking to the ranch. And I'm not letting you take my foreman either."

With a grin, Sheriff Hughes nodded. "I know that."

"What say we all head over to the bunk house and see if St. John has rustled us up some grub and coffee yet?"

There were no protests as Mavrich and the sheriff led the men out of the barn and into the early morning light. Over a good breakfast and steaming cups of coffee, the men talked.

"Think they'll be back here, Mr. Mavrich?" Lloyd asked.

Norman nodded. "Yep. This ranch is too large and tempting for them to give up. Besides, unless they're all yellow, they'll be back just to prove they can take our cattle."

"What about the other ranches?" Maynard wondered. "Think they'll be hit again?"

"The Bar X and the Rising B? Maybe. I wouldn't say any ranch was safe because of the size of it. Would you, Sheriff?"

Sheriff Hughes drained his coffee cup before replying. "Nope. I sure would like to know who's running the gang though. There's something about the way they've been working."

"What do mean, Sheriff?" Hardrich asked.

The sheriff rubbed the back of his neck and frowned. "That's just it. I'm not sure, but something just seems different than any other gang of rustlers I've encountered."

For some time the men sat in silence. Then Norman straightened. "One more cup of coffee, St. John, if you've got any left." He held out his cup as the big ranch cook brought over the coffee pot. "Thanks."

"Mavrich, I'm going to be heading back to town now. Thanks for the food and coffee. Any messages you want me to take?" The sheriff had pushed back his chair and stood, putting his hat back on his head.

"If you'll stop at the manse and let my wife know everything's all right, I'd appreciate it. I'll be in a little later, but I don't want her to worry any longer than she has to. And," Norman added, glancing over at his youngest hand, "stop by the Hearter's place if you would and let his mother and sisters know Lloyd's safe and sound."

The sheriff chuckled. "Sure will. Be seeing you all around." Then he added just before stepping out the door, "And be careful."

There were a few moments of silence after the sheriff's departure and the men waited for Mr. Mavrich to give some orders.

"I know today is Sunday, men," he began, "and I'd like to give you all a full day of rest, but I rather expect the rustlers are waiting for that, and I don't think we ought to oblige them." A murmur of assent passed around the table. "I'm going to have you go out for four hour shifts and I'm sending three of you at a time. That way if something does happen, one can ride back for the rest of us while the other two handle things until we arrive." Mr. Mavrich looked about at the faces of his men. They were all eager and ready to take the first watch.

"Wilson, Burns and Alden, you three get fresh horses, saddle up and head out. Patrol along the southern edge of the ranch but far enough inside that you aren't noticed should our guests decide to return. Split up if you think it best, but don't get out of range for hearing any signal shots. I'll have the next patrol take over for you in four hours. Any questions?"

When the men shook their heads, he nodded towards the door in dismissal. Picking up their rifles and hats, the three chosen men hurriedly left.

As the door shut behind them, Mr. Mavrich continued, "Maynard, Barker and Scott, you three take the next watch. This time, after you take over, if they haven't spotted anything, head to the north line and patrol that."

"What about the far western section, sir?" Maynard asked. "That's the farthest from the ranch and seems to me most likely for any rustlers to set up camp."

Triple Creek's boss nodded thoughtfully. "You've got a point there, but it's a long ride out there and I don't think the cattle have scattered that far. They're probably not much farther than Penny Creek or Crystal Creek. So, for today, stick with the north line."

Maynard nodded. He, Wilson, and Barker may not have been permanent hands on the Triple Creek, but the three men had worked the last two years for Norman Mavrich with the exception of the winter months when they lived in town and did odd jobs for people until spring came once again. Having worked on the ranch before, Maynard respected the boss's decision and didn't question it.

Trying unsuccessfully to hold back a yawn, Mr. Mavrich pushed back his chair. "Well, men, I suggest you get a little shut eye before the next patrol sets off. Hearter and I are heading to town shortly. Lloyd, be ready to leave for church in thirty minutes. Scott, would you mind having the livery horse and Minuet saddled for us then?"

"Sure thing, Boss," Scott nodded.

Glancing down at his dusty clothes, Norman grinned. "I reckon I'd better get cleaned up a bit before heading into town."

Slowly making her way down the street with Mrs. O'Connor, Orlena and Mrs. Kirby, Jenelle couldn't help watching the road which led out of town in the direction of the Triple Creek in hopes of seeing Norman's familiar figure, but she saw nothing. Arriving at the church, the ladies made their way to an empty pew and sat down, though Mrs. Kirby went up to her usual place before the organ. The minutes slowly ticked by and still Norman didn't come. Others gathered, although many of the ranchers had remained away that morning. It was with difficulty that Jenelle refrained from turning her head every time the door opened, and when a slight figure slipped into the seat beside Orlena and a voice whispered, "May I sit with you?" she started.

Turning her head, she saw Charity's pale and somewhat anxious face. "Of course you may, Dear," Jenelle replied in low tones. "But where are your mother and Connie?"

"Mother wasn't feeling well at all this morning. She had a bad spell last night and Connie stayed with her. I came because I thought . . ." her voice trailed off, and she bit her lip.

Reaching across Orlena, Mrs. Mavrich pressed the girl's tightly folded hands. She understood the fear she had for her brother's safety. It was the same fear she had for her husband but had been trying to ignore.

The sound of the organ prevented any further talking and they rose to sing the opening hymn. But, so distracted were their thoughts that the only one who later could have told what the hymn was, was Mrs. O'Connor.

Later, as Reverend Kirby was in the middle of reading his text, the door again opened and the sound of booted feet moving quietly down the aisle could be heard. Orlena heard a faint gasp beside her and glanced up from her Bible to see Norman step past her. As she quickly slid a little closer to Charity so he could sit down, she noticed her friend clinging to the arm of her brother.

Scarcely had Reverend Kirby dismissed the congregation when Jenelle turned to her husband and asked, "What happened? Why were you late? Is everything all right? Did the others come? Oh, Norman, I'm so glad to see you!" and she leaned against him wearily.

"Didn't you get my message?"

Before Jenelle could do more than shake her head, a new voice in the row before them asked, "Mr. Mavrich, where is my husband?"

CHAPTER 10

GREG'S RETURN

Norman looked up. "Mrs. Hughes," he began, "didn't the sheriff return yet? He left over an hour before we did."

Mrs. Hughes shook her head. "I haven't seen him."

Glancing about, Mr. Mavrich noticed Lloyd watching him with a worried frown on his usually cheerful face. Turning to his wife and Mrs. Hughes, he suggested, "Let's move outside. Perhaps he got delayed and has returned now."

However, there was still no sign when they reached the bright sunshine, and the sheriff's deputy came up to ask about him. "He left a good hour before we first started out," Norman repeated.

"What do you mean, first started out?" asked Deputy Travis.

"The horse from the livery threw a shoe just before we reached the road and Hearter would have changed horses, but Scott was able to get the shoe fixed without much trouble. The sheriff left long before we actually got away, and I didn't see any sign of him along the road." He looked questioningly at his hand.

"I didn't either, sir."

"I reckon he met with another rancher and went off to investigate." Norman sounded casual. "I wouldn't start to worry yet, Mrs. Hughes."

"If he doesn't show up soon, Ma," Jonah assured his

mother, "I'll ride out and find him. He's probably got those rustlers pinned down someplace and is just waiting for a few more guns to ride up."

A smile crossed Mrs. Hughes face, and she tousled her son's hair. "You and your imagination," she laughed. "Well," turning to Mr. Mavrich, "if you say not to worry, I won't. I used to be scared stiff any time he was late for a meal or was gone longer than I thought he should be, but I soon realized that it was all a waste of time. I'm sure he has a good reason for not—"

She didn't finish, for at that moment Sheriff Hughes reined up his horse before the church yard and dismounted. "Sorry I'm late for church, Mabel. And Mrs. Mavrich," he touched his hat to her with a grin, "your husband wished me to tell you he'd be right along and everything was all right. And Miss Charity, be sure you tell your mother and sister that your brother is safe and sound."

A relieved laugh went around the small group of people and then his deputy asked, "Well, Sheriff, what took you so long?"

"Oh, Bittner was riding to the Triple Creek to look for me. He was sure he had some rustlers on his place last night too, so I rode back with him to check out the Silver Spur."

"What'd you find?"

"Nothing. Not even a sign of anyone coming onto his land where he claims he saw them. Now, that doesn't mean they weren't there," the sheriff added, "but there wasn't any way I could follow them."

Norman shook his head. "He could be right, Sheriff. With so many of us gone from the ranches yesterday, it would have been a fine time to work several ranches at once, if you had enough men. I'd sure like to know where they're keeping the cattle though." He stopped talking and glanced down at his wife. Noticing her tired though smiling face, he held out his hand to the sheriff, "I'd better be getting back to the ranch now. Thanks for your help last night, Sheriff. Hearter, take your sister home and be sure you're back at the ranch in two hours. And don't ruin Minuet!"

Hearter looked surprised, but then grinned. "Thank you, sir," he began "And don't worry about Minuet. I'll take care of her. Come on, Charity, let's go see Mother and Connie." And they hurried away with Charity taking two steps to each of her brother's long strides.

Before Norman could lead his family over to the livery to hitch up the carriage which had been left there the night before, the Kirby's youngest son was seen driving it towards the church.

Springing down, Quentin Kirby held the horse while Mr. Mavrich assisted the ladies. Then he said, "Mr. Mavrich, could I get a job on your ranch this summer?"

Climbing in and reaching for the reins, Norman eyed the young man from head to toe. "How old are you, son?"

"Fifteen."

"Have you talked with your parents about this yet?"

Quentin shook his head. "Not yet, but I've been doing an awful lot of thinking about a job this summer, and I want to be a rancher."

Hiring a young new hand for the summer hadn't even occurred to Norman and he wasn't prepared to give a direct answer. "Talk it over with your parents, pray about it, and let me know what they say. Then I'll give it some thought. All right?"

The boy looked slightly downcast but answered sturdily enough, "Yes, sir," as he stepped away from the carriage.

That Sunday afternoon at Triple Creek Ranch was one of quiet restfulness. Jenelle, more tired than she knew, had been sent straight to bed by Norman after the noon meal St. John had prepared. Mrs. O'Connor also retired to her room in the early afternoon to rest, leaving Orlena to her own devices, for Norman had, after seeing his wife to her bed, disappeared. For a while Orlena was content to curl up and read, but soon she grew tired and and wandered outside. The air had the smell of sunshine and fresh growing things, and a soft, gentle breeze tickled the small green leaves of the trees, setting them to dancing, while little popcorn clouds hung scattered across the blue bowl of the sky. Breathing deeply, Orlena slowly wandered in the direction of the barn. She had no object in view, and no thought of what she was going to do crossed her mind, so, after gazing for a moment into the dim barn and finding it empty, her feet turned in the direction of the corrals. And like her feet as they wandered here and there, her thoughts wandered from subject to subject without Orlena even realizing it. At last, having reached the small pasture where Lady and Beautiful Dreamer were enjoying the sunshine with a few of the other horses, Orlena climbed up on the bottom rung of the fence and leaned over the top rail.

"I wonder what I would be doing now if I hadn't come here?" she mused half aloud. "I know I certainly wouldn't be standing on a fence looking at some horses!" She smiled to herself at the thought. "I didn't see Elvira or her brother in church this morning. What made them not come? How long will it be before Norman catches the rustlers and who are they? I wonder where Norman is anyway? There will probably be a test in school tomorrow. Perhaps Jenelle will let Charity stay another night with me. I think Mrs. Kirby is pretty, but not as pretty as Jenelle. I wonder if Mother was pretty. I should ask Norman."

"Ask me what?" a voice sounded at her elbow and she turned quickly, nearly falling off the fence. "Sorry," Norman said, as he steadied her. "I didn't mean to startle you. Now, what did you want to ask me?"

For a minute Orlena stood blinking at him with a blank expression on her face, then, as the remembrance of her thoughts came back, she blurted, "Was Mother pretty?"

The question didn't take Norman by surprise and he answered readily enough, "Yep."

"Do you remember her?"

With a nod, he answered softly, "Yes. I can't remember her voice very well, but sometimes when Jenelle laughs, it sounds very much like her laugh."

"What did she look like?" persisted Orlena. "I don't remember her at all. I remember some man with dark hair and a dark mustache tossing me up in the air and laughing, but I don't know who it was."

"Father. You loved it when he would toss you in the air, and he loved listening to your giggle every time he did it. I expect that was why he did it so often."

Moving closer to him, Orlena leaned against the arm Norman was resting over the top rails of the fence and whispered, "Tell me about it."

"I remember Mother sitting in her favorite chair near the window with a bit of sewing in her lap. Her brown hair had come loose from its pins and was falling down around her shoulders in curls much like yours." And Norman glanced down at his sister's dark head. "Her eyes, soft and blue, were full of love as she watched Father romp with you. She laughed at the way you sat on Father's back demanding a "hosey wide," as you called it, until Father was so tired that he lay right down on the floor under you and refused to get up. You tried to get me to play with you then, but I had reading to finish before my lessons the next day and at last you gave up trying to coax me and went to Mother to be cuddled and kissed until it was bed time."

"What happened next?" Orlena begged, as the silence that followed her brother's story grew longer and he seemed to be lost in thought.

"What? Oh." Norman shifted his feet. "That was the last time we all four were together. The accident happened that night, as they were coming home from a concert. Everything changed after that. You went to Grandmother's and I came out here."

"And I wasn't the same when you saw me next?" It was almost a statement.

"Well, not after you had lived with Grandmother for a while," Norman admitted. Then, glancing down at his sister, he smiled and added softly, "I think Mother and Father would be pleased if they saw you now."

Orlena didn't move, but whispered, "What about . . . Grandmother?"

Tipping her face up so he could look into her eyes, Norman assured, "Grandmother would be very pleased." He thought about the note Grandmother Mavrich had written him. "Rescue Orlena from herself." There had been a major difference in Orlena since she had yielded herself to Jesus Christ. True, she wasn't perfect and still had trouble with her temper at times, and with her selfish nature, but no longer was she the spoiled brat Norman had brought to the ranch from the great house in the city.

"Norman! Orlena!"

At the call, Norman grinned and pulled one of his sister's curls lightly. "I think that's the call to supper, and we'd best be moving if we want it."

T

It was Tuesday afternoon and Jenelle was rocking on the porch with her basket of mending beside her when a buggy drove up the lane and stopped before the house. Looking up in surprise, she watched in puzzlement as a nicely dressed man stepped out and then turned and helped a young woman to alight.

"Good afternoon, Mrs. Mavrich," the man called gaily, waving his hat.

"Greg?" Jenelle laid aside the shirt she had been sewing a button on and rose in amazement. "Why, Zacheriah Gregory, when did you arrive? Norman didn't tell me you were coming. We never got a telegram. This must be your wife." And Jenelle held out her hand warmly as the couple came up onto the porch.

"Yes, ma'am," Greg chuckled. "This is Mary. Mary, this is Mrs. Mavrich, the boss's fine wife. But," he added hastily, "she doesn't hold a candle to you. I mean, well, that is—" He stopped in confusion while both ladies laughed.

"He thinks I will be offended if he praises you, Mrs. Mavrich," Mrs. Gregory said with a smile.

"Please, call me Jenelle."

"And you must call me Mary," the English girl replied shyly.

"Did you write, Greg?" Jenelle asked the man who stood looking so uncomfortable and out of place in his city clothes.

"No, we didn't have time. Just decided to catch a train and come on out. Mary thought she'd like to help pick out a house, and we did."

Jenelle blinked. "You did? Already? Where?"

"There was an empty house right next to the Hearter home, and since Mary liked it and I thought it might be nice for Hearter if he knew we were right next door to his mother, especially come winter, we bought it. And it will give Mary someone to talk to when I'm out here working."

"Oh, that house will be just right for you. And I think it will please Lloyd to know someone will be near his mother when Connie is teaching." Jenelle smiled. "But forgive my manners, would you like something to drink?"

Greg shook his head. "No thanks, Mrs. Mavrich. I want to talk to the boss or Hardrich. Where are they?"

"Somewhere out on the range. We've had rustlers around here and they are making a thorough search of the Triple Creek for signs of them." Since Mary had also declined the offered drink, Jenelle motioned her to another rocking chair and sank back into her own. "You are welcome to take a horse and ride out and look for them," she offered the former hand, though she wondered if he could ride with his city clothes on.

"I reckon I'll do just that. If you don't mind that is, Mary?" He looked anxiously at his wife, but when she smiled, he started down the steps, calling back over his shoulder, "I'll be back when I can."

The ladies on the porch watched as he tossed his jacket

and tie into the carriage and strode off towards the barn.

"Oh, dear," Jenelle pressed her hand over her mouth and her eyes twinkled merrily.

"What is it?" Mary asked.

"I don't see how he is going to ride with those clothes and shoes."

Mary smiled. "I told him he should change into what he was accustomed to wearing on the ranch, but he wouldn't listen. If those clothes are ruined, I won't mind. I came over here to marry a cattleman not a finely dressed man from the city. There were plenty of those back home in England."

Just then Mrs. O'Connor stepped out onto the porch and Jenelle introduced her to Greg's new bride. After watching Greg ride away, looking so out of place on the horse in his city clothes that all the ladies laughed, Jenelle picked up her mending once more.

"I hope you don't mind if I keep working, Mary," she smiled. "I always seem to have socks to darn or clothes to mend."

"Do let me help," begged Mary eagerly. "Since I've arrived I've hardly gotten to sew a stitch of anything, for it was all done for me in the city."

"Do you like buttons?"

"I adore sewing on buttons!" was the unexpected answer.

"Then you may have the pleasure." Quickly Jenelle handed over the shirt in her hands and picked up something else. "Norman is very hard on his buttons and is always pulling them off when he gets in a hurry, and Orlena seems to be following his ways."

Mrs. O'Connor, having finished the work indoors, brought out another chair and joined the circle with her knitting.

CHAPTER 11

PATIENT HELP

"I won't let Mrs. O'Connor touch my mending basket," Jenelle explained with a merry laugh. "For if I once let her get started, she would finish it and I would be left with nothing to do."

"Soon you won't have time for your mending basket," Mrs. O'Connor predicted with a knowing look.

Smiling, with a soft glow in her eyes, Jenelle replied, "Then it can all pile up and wait for me. Really, Mrs. O'Connor, you have been wonderful and I don't know what we would have done without you these past months, but my mending basket is my mending basket." Then changing the subject, she asked, "Mary, did you get to meet the Hearters?"

"Only Mrs. Hearter. I understand that Connie teaches school."

"Yes, and Charity would have been in school. Lloyd works here on the ranch, one daughter is married, and another is living with an aunt and uncle and attending school in one of the larger cities. But, how did you happen to get to know Greg?"

And so the subject changed once again and the talk flowed on as talk will, while nimble fingers flew and the minutes slipped away into hours. It wasn't until Orlena arrived home from school that Mrs. O'Connor rose to begin preparing the evening meal. Mary looked out over the fields where her husband had ridden off and a slightly anxious look crept over her face. "Do you think Greg will be back soon?" she asked. "We should be getting back to town so that I can begin preparing supper."

"I hope you and Greg will stay and have supper with us tonight," Jenelle invited. "I really don't know when he'll be getting back, but I do know that Mrs. O'Connor is making plenty of food. We would love to have you stay."

Graciously Mary accepted, provided, of course, that her husband didn't mind.

Supper was nearly ready and Orlena was setting the table, when Norman and Greg rode up with Davis and Hearter.

"I wonder where the others are?" Jenelle remarked, tying a last knot and snipping the thread. "If St. John isn't coming until later, I should tell Orlena to set two more places. Excuse me for a minute, Mary."

Mrs. Gregory nodded and carefully folded the last shirt.

A few minutes later, when Norman and Greg approached the porch, Jenelle had returned and picked up her mending basket. Greg introduced his wife to Mr. Mavrich. Then, after greeting her husband, Jenelle turned to Greg. "You are staying for supper, aren't you?"

Norman began to laugh. "I told you my wife would be expecting you and your wife to eat supper here, Greg." Then he turned to Jenelle. "Hearter and Davis will be eating with us tonight as the others are spending the night on the range with the cattle."

"I already had Orlena set two extra places."

The evening meal was an enjoyable one, but the new couple didn't remain long afterwards as Greg wanted to return to the hotel before it was dark. "Our things should be coming in on the train tomorrow," he assured Mr. Mavrich. "And by the end of the week we should be settled in and I can come to work. But," he added quickly, "if you need me before then, let me know and I can come."

"Next Monday should be just fine, Greg, as that's when Tompkins will be joining us again." Mr. Mavrich stepped back from the carriage and nodded as Greg touched the reins to the horse's back.

"Good bye!" Jenelle called with a wave.

Standing together in the yard, Mr. and Mrs. Mavrich watched the carriage until it turned onto the road leading to town. Wearily, Jenelle leaned her head against her husband's shoulder.

"Tired, Sweet?" Norman's arm had encircled her waist and he dropped a kiss on her hair.

"Yes, but it was good to see Greg again and meet Mary. She really is sweet. Norman, I wish I could go help Mary get settled in and introduce her around town."

"Absolutely not," came the emphatic reply. "But it's just like you to think of it, Darling," he added.

With a little sigh, Jenelle murmured, "I'll be glad when I can do something again."

Pulling her close, Norman hugged her and asked, "Don't you call making me the happiest man on earth, doing anything?"

It was hard to tell if Jenelle blushed at Norman's words or not, for the sun was setting and cast a rosy glow over everything as the master of Triple Creek Ranch stooped and kissed his wife.

Orlena looked up from her books as her brother and sister entered the dining room a little while later. "Norman," she begged, "won't you please make this figure straighten out?"

Stepping over, Norman leaned over her shoulder. "Which one?"

Orlena pointed to a long column of figures on the slate before her.

"What's wrong with it?"

"The numbers are always changing because I get a different answer every time I do it, and I don't know which one is right!" Orlena was tired and had been working on that same arithmetic problem for at least five minutes.

Pulling out the chair beside her, Norman sat down. "Let me see it."

Gladly Orlena shoved the slate before him and leaned her head on her hand.

"This shouldn't be hard, Sis, it's just simple addition."

Heaving a long sigh, Orlena replied, "It shouldn't be hard, but it is. I haven't gotten the same answer twice, and I've tried adding from the top to the bottom and then from the bottom up. Can't you tell me if it's right?"

"It's not."

Orlena groaned dismally. "Maybe I'll just skip that problem and work on my paper." She was reaching for her pencil when her brother's hand was placed on hers.

"Isn't that paper due at the end of the week?" he asked. When Orlena nodded, Norman said quietly, "Then it can wait. Finish your arithmetic problems first."

For a moment Orlena made no move to try the problem on her slate again. She knew she would get the answer wrong and she was so tired of those numbers, yet she had asked for her brother's help. Reluctantly she took the slate pencil and bent her head over those bewildering figures. When at last she thought she had the correct answer, she wrote it down and looked up. "Is that right?"

"Check it and see," was the unsatisfactory reply.

"Norman!" Orlena wailed, almost in despair. "I can't add those up again! They won't come out the same. Won't you just tell me, please?"

But Norman shook his head. "I can't do your work for you, but I will stay here and make sure the numbers don't change while you work." He smiled as he spoke, but Orlena was too close to tears to see it.

Since she was already sure she wouldn't get the same answer, it wasn't a surprise when she wrote down the number and saw it was different. "I told you I couldn't do it," she cried as the tears began to fall and she started to rub out the answers.

"Wait a minute," Norman chided, stopping her hand and pulling the slate away from her falling tears. "Orlena, look at your answers again."

Somewhat bewildered, she brushed the tears away and looked down. "They're different," she complained.

"Yes, but look at what is different. See, you forgot to carry the ten on this row and so, of course, the answer was different." Norman pointed to the two answers as he spoke.

For a moment Orlena stared, then hesitantly she redid her second answer and saw with amazement that it was the same as the first. "Is it really the right answer?"

"Yes, it really is," Norman affirmed. "Now, how many more do you have to do?"

"Only one and it shouldn't be so hard. But that doesn't mean you can leave yet," she hastened to say before her brother could rise. "I may need help again." However, Norman's help was not needed, for the numbers didn't shift around, allowing Orlena to discover the correct answer the first time.

Not being able to keep back a yawn, Norman rose and said, "Suppose you work on your paper tomorrow, Sis. It's growing late."

Not minding in the least, Orlena thanked her brother for his help and gathered her books. She herself was yawning and the thought of being done with her homework was appealing. After bidding Jenelle and Norman good night, she carried her books up to her room before slipping down the hall to Mrs. O'Connor's room.

A light tap on the half open door caused Mrs. O'Connor to look up and beckon. "Come in, Child," she invited with a warm smile.

Obeying the invitation, Orlena pushed open the door and stepped inside. "Mrs. O'Connor," she began, perching herself on the edge of the bed, "can you think of anything that Charity and I can do to help Elvira?"

"Help her do what?"

Orlena frowned a little and tucked one foot up under her while she fingered the tucks on her dress. "Well, she's miserable, she doesn't really have any friends, and I think she'd like to join us sometimes, but she won't. And it's not even because she has a nice dress on like I used to wear to school before I got sensible. She wears the same kind of clothes the rest of us wear and she won't join us in games unless Miss Hearter makes her."

"Have you asked her?"

"Yes. She used to ignore us, at least she ignored me, but now she just refuses."

The older woman rocked for a few minutes without speaking and at last said, "Aye, tis not an easy life to live without the Lord, Orlena. I think the best thing for you and Charity to do to help Elvira is to pray for her and look for ways to be kind to her. Perhaps instead of joining in the games tomorrow at recess, you could join Elvira."

"And just sit and stare?"

Mrs. O'Connor laughed softly. "No, talk. Don't talk at her, but with her. Include her as much as you can in your conversation. Have you invited her to the sewing bee on Saturday?"

Orlena shook her head. "I wasn't sure how she would get there if her mother didn't come."

"Perhaps her father will be well enough entirely to allow both the ladies of the family to attend. But it wouldn't hurt to invite her anyway."

Swinging her foot, Orlena stared down at her hands and said, "I suppose I should."

"Don't you want her to come?" Mrs. O'Connor stopped rocking to look searchingly at the girl before her. "Orlena," her voice was quiet, "if you really want to help Elvira, you can't just try to help her during school hours and pray for her a few times during the week. You must be willing to make an effort any time you have an opportunity, and your prayers must be sincere. The Lord said in His Word that the effectual fervent prayer of a righteous man availeth much."

Looking up, Orlena smiled faintly. She rose. "Thank you, Mrs. O'Connor. I'll try. I do want Elvira to be a Christian. I know she would be so much happier. Good night." Then she slowly and quietly made her way back to her own room and prepared for bed. She remembered a verse she had found a few days before, which her mother had marked. It began, "Love is patient, love is kind."

"I haven't been very patient yet," she thought, remembering how long she herself had held aloof from the very love and friendship she was now trying to offer Elvira Ledford.

"I'll invite her to the sewing bee tomorrow," she decided a few minutes later as she rose from her knees and climbed into bed. "Of course, all the ladies and girls were already invited, but maybe if I say something to her she'll try to come. Perhaps she'll let Charity and me eat with her." With her mind trying to think of other ways to be kind to Elvira, she fell asleep.

☨

Two days later Norman entered the kitchen with a quick step and his mouth in a firm line. "Sorry, Jenelle, I don't have time for breakfast this morning."

Jenelle turned from the stove in surprise. "Not have time for breakfast?" she repeated, staring at her husband. "What's happened?"

"Greg just rode in with word that several fences have been cut on the Bar X and cattle pushed through. One of the hands rode in for the sheriff. Somehow Greg heard and rode out to tell me."

She didn't ask how Greg knew about the help Norman had been giving the Ledfords, or how he had managed to hear the news so early in the morning, instead she asked, "Are you taking any of the men with you?"

He nodded. "Tracy, Wilson and Burns. Davis is sticking around the ranch buildings, if you should need him for anything. Hardrich will have the others out on the range. Don't know when I'll be back, but don't work too hard or worry."

"I'll be careful if you will too." She looked up bravely and smiled. She knew Norman was worried about her, and she didn't want him to be.

Snatching up a few biscuits from a plate, Norman kissed her and was gone, leaving Jenelle standing with a bowl and spoon in her hands looking at the door.

CHAPTER 12

PRANKSTERS OR RUSTLERS?

"Jenelle," Orlena's voice caused her to start and turn back to the stove. "I have the eggs, but I saw Norman and several others riding off. Where are they going? Did they eat breakfast already? Why did they leave?"

Setting the bowl down on the table, Jenelle sighed and tucked a strand of hair back before she replied. "Someone cut some fences at the Bar X and Norman is taking some of the men to see if they can help out."

"Without breakfast?"

Jenelle nodded. "Sometimes ranchers don't have time for things like breakfast, Orlena. But come, you and Mrs. O'Connor must be hungry, and we can eat."

"Let's eat in here," Orlena suggested, noticing her sister looked tired, though she was sure she hadn't been up many hours. "Mrs. O'Connor won't mind."

Mrs. O'Connor didn't mind, and before long the meal was over and Orlena ran for her school books, waved good bye and started off for town.

Hurrying along the road, it wasn't long before Orlena caught up with Flo and Jenny Carmond. "Hello," she greeted them with a smile. The neighbors were quickly becoming friends.

Both girls returned the greeting warmly and Jenny asked, "Have the kittens grown?"

Orlena shrugged. "I don't know. I haven't seen them since last week when Charity and I found the nest. The mother moved them, and I haven't found it yet."

"I wish I could find them," Jenny sighed. "Our cat is too old to have kittens any more and it would be such fun to find a nest again."

"Do you think you could come over after school? We could all look for them," Orlena proposed eagerly. "Maybe Charity could come too, but," she added slowly, "she probably can't come on account of having to get back home again." She kicked a rock off the road and then added as she saw Jenny's face fall, "But you could come anyway, couldn't you?"

"I think so," Flo answered. "We could stop at the house on the way and make sure. But come on, we'd better hurry or we'll be late."

The bright morning sun shone down on the three girls as they hurried into town, down the road and into the school yard, calling greetings to their friends or talking eagerly together. The air was fresh and invigorating and, for many, the thought of spending the day inside the schoolhouse wasn't appealing.

Over at the Bar X, the men were working hard trying to gather the cattle which had gone through the cut fence, checking the rest of the fence line for other cuts and then, once the cattle were back on Bar X land, fixing the fences. Elbert was thankful when Mr. Mavrich and his hands rode in, for the sheriff had been out at another ranch and hadn't arrived yet. The three Triple Creek hands got right to work with the others.

"What exactly happened, Elbert?" Norman asked as the young boss rode over to meet him.

Elbert shook his head, pulling off his hat and wiping his face on his sleeve. "One of the hands was out patrolling and surprised whoever was doing it. He said there were at least two men on horseback, and he shot at them, but they didn't return the fire, and he couldn't see where they went. Then he rode in to get Johnson, and Johnson sent some other men out and woke me." He shook his head and watched as a young steer was roped and almost dragged back through the fence. "I just wish I knew who would pull a stunt like this."

"I don't think it was just a prank, Elbert," Mr. Mavrich said quietly. "Of course, I could be mistaken, but—" he left the rest of his sentence unfinished as Johnson rode up.

"Anything happen to the other fence lines?" Elbert inquired quickly.

Johnson nodded. "Two other places the fences were down on this side of the ranch. Edgar has some men out checking the other sides, but, unless it was a large group of troublemakers, I don't think the other side'll have been touched. And there weren't any cattle out," he added. "And we fixed the fences."

"Johnson," Norman asked, "who do you think did this?"

The foreman shook his head. "I don't know. Rustlers wouldn't work this way, and their running away when just one man with a gun shows up makes me think it was a prank."

"Mr. Mavrich doesn't think so," Elbert countered, and his foreman turned in surprise.

"You don't, Mavrich? Why?"

Norman hesitated. "I'm not sure why yet, but something doesn't feel right."

Further conversation was discontinued then as some of the cattle were giving trouble about returning to their own pastures and the three men rode out to lend a hand. It took quite a bit of persuasion to drive the rest of the herd back through the fence, but at last, after a good bit of work, the final stubborn steer started through and was quickly followed by the cattlemen.

Dismounting, Mr. Mavrich lent a hand in fixing the fence and making sure the wires were tight. Once that was done, he strode over to where some of the men were gathered about their young boss and foreman talking, and he quietly listened.

"I know there were at least two of them," one hand was saying. "I just wish it had been light enough for me to see 'em!"

"Wonder where the sheriff is?" another added.

"What can the sheriff do?" Clint Johnson asked. "It's not like we've got something for him to go off of."

Noticing Norman Mavrich standing on the outskirts of the men, Elbert circled around the group. "Mr. Mavrich," he said quietly, "thanks for your help. I know you're busy at the Triple Creek, and your taking time to come out here means a lot to me and the men."

Norman waved his thanks away with a smile and changed the subject. "How did your father take the news?"

A look of worry or at least concern flickered across the young man's face for a moment and then was gone. "I didn't tell him. I didn't even tell Mother. Perhaps I was wrong, but I didn't want to worry them and I knew Pa would have insisted on getting out of bed."

"Well, you didn't lose any cattle and things are taken care of. Now, unless you think you still need our assistance, my men and I had better be heading back to the ranch. I reckon the sheriff will be along shortly. And Elbert," he added before mounting his horse, "let me know if you need extra help for the round-up."

"I will. Thank you, sir."

Burns, Tracy and Wilson had also mounted and with a word of farewell, the four men turned and rode off at a steady lope.

A few miles from the Bar X they encountered Sheriff Hughes heading for the ranch. He stopped and asked what was going on. Norman told him in a few words and then asked, "Where were you, Sheriff?"

"Harrington sent word that he had rustlers at his place and off I rode to the Lucky Shoe."

"Find anything?"

"No! I tell you, Mavrich, these rustlers have got to be stopped! They seem to know everything that's going on."

"What do you mean?" Norman leaned forward and rested an arm on the saddle horn. "I mean that Harrington had let most of his men have a holiday last evening and that's when we figure they were hit. Lost a dozen good beef steers too. Now this at the Bar X, . . . could be the work of a couple troublemakers with a desire to do mischief." The sheriff suddenly eyed Norman's face keenly and said, "You don't think so, Mavrich?"

Straightening up, Norman shook his head. "Can't say why, yet, sir, but give me a little time. I may be able to make two and two equal four."

With raised eyebrows at the rancher's cryptic words, Sheriff Hughes nodded. "Just don't take too long or every ranch in the area will have lost cattle. But I'd best be on my way. I'll come by your place later for an explanation of those words, Deputy."

Giving a nod, Norman and his men started off again. No one spoke, though the three cowhands couldn't help wondering what their boss was thinking. When they neared Rough Rock, Norman spoke.

"You men head back to the ranch and tell Mrs. Mavrich or Mrs. O'Connor that I was detained in town a little bit. I don't think I'll be long, but I can't say for sure."

"Right, sir," Burns replied, nodding.

Turning Captain's head down the main street, Norman rode slowly, almost casually, watching every person he saw with keen interest from under the wide brim of his hat. The number of people out and about diminished as he turned onto another street. At last, having reached a little house, he dismounted and strode up to the door. Before he had a chance to knock, however, the door was opened and Mrs. Gregory stood before him with a smile.

"Welcome, Mr. Mavrich, to our little home. Greg will be pleased you called. Do step inside. Would you like something to drink?"

Removing his hat as he stepped inside, Norman shook his head. "No, thank you, ma'am. I can't stay. I just wanted to see Greg a minute about something."

"He's—"

"Right here," Greg finished, stepping into the room. "Mr. Mavrich, what brings you here?"

"Rustlers. While you are in town, keep your eyes and ears open for any stray word someone might drop, or for any strangers in town. I think they've got an inside man here and we've got to find something and soon!"

Greg's eyes lit up. "Sure thing, Boss. I'll try to find something out. Should I tell you or the sheriff what I discover?"

"Either. Or Deputy Travis. But Greg, watch yourself. Don't get mixed up with Con Blomberg again."

Chuckling, Greg assured, "Don't worry, Boss. I've got a wife now, and I've had my fill of Blomberg."

"Huh," Norman snorted. "Just see to it that you keep your eyes open. I have to get back to the ranch now." He opened the door and, seeing a man slowly strolling past in the street, added, "Then I'll see you on Monday, Greg. Mrs. Greg, thank you for your hospitality." With a nod to the couple in the door, he swung up on Captain and started down the street. He knew he had seen that man before. But who was he?

Although Norman thought hard as he rode back through town, he still could not recall who the man was he had seen. "Perhaps I've never met him but only seen him," he thought as he left town. "But where would I have seen him, and why was he walking so slowly down that street?" He tried a trick he had learned from a schoolmate in college of trying to picture the man next to each person he could remember. Often this little trick had helped him connect one person with another, but this time, though he tried every rancher for miles around, every shop keeper and businessman in town, he was no closer to making a connection when he turned into Triple Creek's lane then he had been when he left town.

Drawing rein before the barn, Norman noticed a strange horse tied to a fence. Quickly dismounting, Norman looped Captain's reins loosely over a rail and walked towards the house, his sharp eyes noticing that there was no sign of Wilson, Burns or Tracy and that Mack Davis was also not around. With a frown, he sprang to the porch and opened the door, calling, "Jenelle!"

CHAPTER 13

A BIG MISTAKE

"Norman, you're home. Look who is here!"

A tall, lanky man rose from the table and turned. His face was pleasant and there was a grin on his face as Norman stared blankly at him a moment. "Howdy, Mavrich," the man said.

"Bruce? Edmund Bruce! What on earth are you doing here? I thought you were in California." Norman was warmly shaking hands with his visitor as he spoke. "What brings you to the Triple Creek Ranch?"

The man laughed but turned to Jenelle. "I tell you, Mrs. Mavrich, this husband of yours asks more questions at a time than anyone I know. And he expects them all answered."

Tossing his hat on the table, Norman grinned, kissed his wife and replied, "She already knew that. But tell me what you're doing here, Bruce. You're staying for supper, and no arguments."

Mrs. O'Connor set a glass of water before the returned ranch boss and said, "Sure and tis a late invitation yer offering with yer wife already tellin' him he was stayin' and him accepting."

Lifting his glass, Norman said, "By the way, Jenelle, where is Davis?"

"I'm not sure. He was here when Mr. Bruce rode in."

"Probably around somewhere then. Now, Bruce, what

are you doing here?"

The newcomer had resumed his seat when Norman sat down. "Well, I was looking for work and, passing through this area, I thought it would be a shame if I didn't pay you a visit and see if you, or anyone else in these parts, was hiring these days. Wasn't sure if your outfit was still as large as rumor had it back when your uncle was alive. After all, it's been a few years since our college days, and a lot can happen in that time." His face grew sober and he traced the grain of wood on the table as he continued in a quieter voice. "I was in California for a few years and buried my wife out there and my son. With them gone I had no desire to remain, so I went south and worked punching cattle in New Mexico for a while. Then I moved on. I've been here and there, doing odd jobs in towns and on farms or ranches, but I haven't found a place I could really settle. Then, a few days ago, I was reading my Bible and a letter you had written me fell out. It wasn't until then that I realized how close I was to this ranch, and I decided that even if I didn't get work around here, I wanted to see you again and get a glimpse of the Triple Creek Ranch." His smile had returned as he finished and then added, "There you have it, Mavrich. My life in five minutes."

In a voice that was quiet, Norman said, "I'm glad you came."

"So am I. Are you hiring?"

Norman didn't answer but stared thoughtfully into space, and his fingers began to drum the top of the table.

"Uh, oh," Mr. Bruce grinned. "I remember that sound. Mrs. Mavrich, your husband used to drive us crazy with that finger tapping of his when he had some hard thinking to do back in college."

Jenelle smiled and looked at her husband.

Straightening suddenly, Norman reached for his hat and said, "Jenelle, Bruce and I are going out for a bit. I'd like to show him some of the ranch. We'll be back in time for supper though. And," he added, rising, "St. John'll be back with some of the men, and they'll eat in the bunkhouse. So, it's just the family tonight. Come on, Bruce."

Forcing a frown on his merry face, Bruce sighed dismally and remarked, "He's already sending me out to eat with the hands. Withdrawing his invitation for supper all because I asked for a job. Ho, hum. Well, so long, Mrs. Mavrich, Mrs. O'Connor. It was nice meeting you both and—"

"I did no such thing," Norman retorted, punching his friend lightly on the shoulder. "You know you've always been like the brother I never had. Now let's get going."

Leaving the ladies laughing in the kitchen, the two men strolled outside together and over to the barn.

"Is this a walking tour or do we get to ride?" Bruce asked.

"We ride."

It wasn't until the men had mounted and ridden for a few minutes that Bruce broke the silence. "Fine place you have here, Mavrich. But what's the trouble?"

"Trouble?" Norman glanced over at his companion. "What are you talking about?"

"Now don't give me that. It may have been years since college, but I can still tell when you've got something on your mind. And I don't mean the price of beef in the fall."

Pulling up beside a little rivulet which often found its way from Crystal Creek in the spring, Norman glanced around quietly before turning his keen grey eyes on his friend's face. The other met the steady, searching gaze with one of frank honesty and Norman began. "All right. There has been trouble with cattle rustlers the past few weeks. Three ranches have lost cattle, and strangers were on the Triple Creek a few days ago, but as far as we can tell, we haven't lost any cattle. The sheriff and I think it may either be an inside group or at least that they have an inside man working with them."

"Why do you say that?"

"This outfit seems to know when there are fewer hands on the ranch and what ones are small or spread out. This morning there was a ranch with fences cut and another ranch in the opposite direction which lost some cattle."

"And you think they were the same group?" Bruce interrupted.

Norman nodded and waited.

After a minute, his friend began to nod. "I can see how that could work for a rustler's advantage. Do you suspect anyone in town?"

"I don't know. I'm not in town much and even if I were, I'm too well known for any loose tongues to talk around me. If you're looking for work . . ."

"I could go play the part of a drifter in town, is that what you were getting at?"

A faint smile crossed Norman's face. "Something like that. Every hand I've got is known to work for me. You on the other hand—"

"Are a complete stranger and might get in where others would be barred." Taking his hat off and letting the light, late afternoon breeze blow through his reddish-blond hair, Edmund Bruce sat motionless on his horse and stared out across the green fields. From somewhere a meadowlark sang, and a rabbit hopped from under a small bush and began to nibble the leaves of a dandelion. "I'm not sure I'll discover anything," he said at last, turning to his waiting friend. "But I'm willing to give it a try, as long as your sheriff doesn't throw me in the lock-up for hanging around town."

"I'll make sure he knows you're working on the right side of the law," Norman assured, his face sober.

"This really has you worried, doesn't it?" Bruce had grown serious at the sight of his friend's face and he reached out a hand and placed it on Norman's arm. "You aren't going to find and catch rustlers by growing worried. You've got to keep your head, Mavrich. What do you say we pray about it right now?"

Drawing a deep breath after the prayer, Norman looked up. He could feel half the load gone from his shoulders. "You are an answer to prayer, Bruce. I'm very glad you came."

A grin came back across the newcomer's face, and he replied, "So'm I. But, Mavrich, I'm beginning to grow powerful tired of looking at this bit of water. What say we ride on?"

During supper that evening, and afterwards as the family sat around the fire, Norman and his friend told stories of their college days and of some of the scrapes they had found themselves in. Mrs. O'Connor and Jenelle often shook their heads in the midst of their laughter, and Orlena finally asked, "Didn't you ever have to study?"

"Study?" Mr. Bruce exclaimed. "My dear young lady, your brother didn't need to study. All he needed was to tap his fingers and every word he read came flooding back and he knew the answers. I tried it once, but it took too much thought to keep my fingers tapping, so I never could remember the answers."

Feeling certain that Mr. Bruce was teasing her, Orlena smiled, but sighed, "I wish I could tap my fingers and remember my arithmetic."

Her brother turned to look at her. "I'm sorry, Sis. I should have asked sooner; do you have much homework tonight?"

With a shake of her head Orlena replied, "Only finishing my paper."

As he glanced out the window at the dark sky, the clock chimed the hour and Norman rose. "I didn't realize it was so late. Orlena, how long will it take you to finish that paper?"

"It shouldn't take very long."

"Then you'd better get to it. I'm going to check things in the barn and speak to the men about tomorrow. Bruce, would you like to join me?" When he received an affirming nod from his guest, Mr. Mavrich rose. "We'll be back in a little while, Jenelle," he smiled down at his wife who was busy sewing.

The following morning before Orlena left for school, she was cautioned not to mention Mr. Bruce to anyone or even act like she knew him, if she should see him in town. "Don't even tell Charity about him," Norman warned. "For all you or anyone else knows, he's a complete stranger."

Though she didn't understand the necessity for those instructions, she promised to comply and started off. Mr. Bruce hadn't eaten breakfast with them or even been seen by Orlena, and she wondered where he was.

The truth was that he and Norman had decided it would be best if he left the ranch before it was daylight so that no one would notice he had been at the Triple Creek. Norman had watched his friend ride off into the dusky morning, thankful that he had come and praying that something would happen soon to uncover the rustlers.

"Mavrich! Mr. Mavrich!"

The sudden and unexpected shout brought Norman out of the barn in an instant and he caught the bridle of a winded horse. "Alden, what is it? What's happened?" he demanded of the rider.

"Hardrich sent me to find you, sir," Alden gasped. "We just now discovered them."

"Rustlers?"

"No, sir, Bar X, Silver Spur and Rising B cattle! On the Triple Creek Ranch, sir! Nearly sixty head."

"What?" Norman's face registered his shock. "Where?"

"Just past Penny Creek, sir. We were checking the area and Hearter spotted the first one and then we began finding others. That's when Hardrich sent me to tell you."

For half a minute the owner of the Triple Creek Ranch stood in thought, a frown on his face. Then he let go of the bridle and ordered, "Dismount. Scott!" he shouted over his shoulder.

"Right here, sir," Scott answered. He had also heard the shouts and had come from the corral in time to hear Alden's story.

"Take care of Alden's mount. Alden, bring Arrow and get him saddled while I saddle Captain."

Moments later both horses were saddled and the two men were ready for some fast riding to the pasture by Penny Creek. "Scott, see to it that no word of this goes beyond the barn. Tell Mrs. Mavrich I've had to ride out for a while and don't know when I'll be back."

"Yes, sir," Scott nodded, offering no comment about what had happened and then watching the two men gallop off across the fields.

Arriving at Penny Creek, Mr. Mavrich and Alden urged their horses carefully across the full stream and up the other bank. In another minute they could see cattle and horsemen and, kicking their horses into a run, covered the last of the ground in a hurry.

The men were obviously excited and had been talking and speculating about what had happened, but all fell silent when the boss rode up. Norman didn't say a word as he slowly rode Captain among the cattle, his eyes noting the three distinctive brands on the hides of the animals.

"Have you gone over this entire area?" he asked his foreman.

"Sure have. We've combed it twice and this is what we've found that isn't ours." Jim Hardrich looked from the cattle peacefully grazing to Mr. Mavrich, and waited.

"Is there any sign of a break in the fences?" was Norman's next quick question.

"No, sir," Maynard replied quickly. "Burns and I just finished checking and there's no sign anywhere along here."

"The Bar X and Rising B knew they had lost cattle. I haven't heard anything about Silver Spur missing any though," Mr. Mavrich mused. "But they're rather large and might not notice."

"Do you want someone to ride for the sheriff?" Hardrich asked.

But Norman shook his head. "No, I think we need to keep this quiet. I'll let Bates, Bittner and Elbert know we've got some of their cattle, but I don't want the rustlers knowing. I'm going to need an accurate count of each brand, men," he directed, nodding at the cattle.

The hands set at once to sort and count the cattle from each ranch, leaving the foreman and ranch boss alone together.

"What do you aim to do with these cattle?" Hardrich questioned.

"Nothing. I'm going to let them graze where they like and mingle with ours all they want. I'm hoping the rustlers will try planting a few others on the ranch and we can catch them. I reckon we can sort them out come branding time. Hardrich, have you noticed we were missing any cattle?"

After taking a drink from his canteen, the foreman replied, "Not that I could tell, but I reckon we could be missing about the same number as we have extras."

"That's what I was thinking. We've got to find out where they're keeping the cattle they're taking!" And Norman slapped his leg. "If we weren't so busy and if Jenelle . . ." he paused and looked back in the direction of the ranch house. "I'd gather a posse and wouldn't stop until I had hunted them to their lair." His eyes were flashing steel and his jaw was set. "They've made a big mistake if they think they can try to pull anything over on this ranch. A big mistake. Now, here's my plan . . ."

CHAPTER 14

"SEND HIM SOON"

Morning had passed, and it was early afternoon before Norman returned to the ranch house to check on his wife before heading out to visit some of the other ranches. Entering the front room he stopped and then, quickly crossing the room, scolded gently, "Jenelle Mavrich, what are you doing?" He lifted her from the stool she was standing on and set her down on the sofa. "You know you are to take things easy right now."

With a wet cloth in one hand, Jenelle laughed. "I am taking things easy," she protested. "I'm only washing the inside of these windows. The outsides really need washing, but I'll let you or one of the hands do that."

"You washed these windows last week," Norman protested, taking her cloth and tossing it into her pail of water. "They can't be dirty again already."

"But they are and the ladies are coming to sew tomorrow and—"

"And I took away your playthings," Norman finished for her with a smile. When she nodded, he sighed and shook his head. "All right. But please, Sweet, don't try to wash anything higher than you can reach from the floor, or I won't feel that I can leave you."

Instantly Jenelle's face sobered, and she asked, "Where are you going?"

"I have to visit a few ranches about something. But I should be back for supper. Scott is in the yard or the corrals working, if you should need him for anything."

"But what if I need you?"

"I'll be at the Silver Spur, then the Rising B, and then I've got to head over to the Bar X. I'll be as quick as I can though," he promised.

Jenelle nodded and, after returning his kiss, remained where she was until the water in her pail had grown cold and she had lost all desire to wash the windows. They really weren't very dirty, and if Norman was going to worry about her, they could just wait. "Why don't we have cleaning bees?" she wondered aloud.

"Just think how nice it would be to have ladies coming over to spring clean the house." Then Jenelle burst into laughter. "And every one of us would be busy days before the others came, cleaning it ourselves." She chuckled again and rose somewhat stiffly to make her way to the kitchen.

Slowly, Orlena opened the kitchen door and stepped inside. Her sober face and drooping shoulders told Mrs. O'Connor that something wasn't right.

"And how was school today, Orlena?" she asked briskly as she bustled around the kitchen.

"Fine." Without another word, Orlena trudged into the dining room and up the stairs to her room. School had been fine, but her invitation to Elvira hadn't gone so well. She had asked her at recess about coming to the sewing bee, but Elvira had only looked at her with a superior expression and then turned away. It had taken the rest of the time at school for her to gather up enough courage to press her invitation again once school was dismissed. Summoning up her courage, she had approached Elvira.

"Elvira, I wanted to make sure you knew that you and your mother are invited to the sewing bee tomorrow. Won't you please come?"

Her only reply was a toss of the head and a short, "I'm

much too busy to spend a day sewing for rich snobs." And she had walked away with a sniff.

Charity had stood beside her friend, unsure of what to say.

Now, alone in her room, Orlena sat on her bed and thought about it. Why had Elvira said what she had? Blinking back tears, she changed out of her school dress and slowly went out to take care of the chickens. Why was it so hard to be friends with Elvira? Most of the other children at school had accepted Orlena as one of themselves, but not Elvira Ledford. Orlena couldn't help but wonder if the problem lay in the fact that she had been unable to return the dime novels she had borrowed before winter. Norman had discovered them and had consigned them all to the fire.

How long she stood there watching the chickens, Orlena didn't know, but at last, as the sound of an approaching horse roused her, she became aware of the lateness of the day and soberly turned toward the house.

Supper was a quiet meal that night in the ranch house. Norman and Orlena were both preoccupied, each with their own troubles, while Jenelle, feeling tired, was more silent than usual. Not usually one to talk much, Mrs. O'Connor let the stillness continue until at last Norman roused himself and glanced at his sister. "How was school today, Orlena?"

"Fine." Her eyes remained on her plate and she slowly took another bite.

Realizing that Orlena hadn't said more than a few words since she had returned from school, Jenelle asked, "Did Elvira say if she and her mother were coming tomorrow?"

Orlena shrugged and pushed the last of her supper around on her plate.

"What is that supposed to mean, Sis?" Norman could tell something wasn't right, but he had been so busy with the affairs of the ranch and the cattle rustlers that he didn't recall at once the ongoing trouble between the two girls. "Did she say they were coming?"

Again Orlena lifted her shoulders. "May I be excused, please?" And at Jenelle's nod, she rose and quickly carried her dishes to the kitchen without another word.

With a bewildered frown Norman turned to Jenelle. "What was that about?"

"I'm guessing that Elvira didn't tell Orlena if she was coming tomorrow or not. Did she say anything to you, Mrs. O'Connor?"

The housekeeper shook her head and also rose. "Perhaps she'll tell me what is going on if you two stay out of the kitchen," she said.

This Norman was only too glad to do, and the couple retired to the front room. Norman offered to build a fire, but Jenelle shook her head. She felt warm enough without one and settled down in her rocking chair while he began to slowly pace the room, arms folded and an almost stern look on his face.

After watching him for a minute, Jenelle asked softly, "Are you worried about me, the ranch, or the rustlers?"

"Huh?" Norman stopped and stared. "Oh, I'm not exactly worried about anything, I'm just thinking. Sometimes, Jenelle, I feel that all I ever do these days is think, think and think again. We've got to find those rustlers and figure out who is tipping them off in town and discover where they are keeping the stolen cattle before things get worse."

"There haven't been any clues?"

"Not one. But I'm praying something will break in town and at least give us a lead to who is behind the whole thing." Norman had stridden over to the window and unconsciously placed his foot on the stool Jenelle had been using earlier when she was washing the windows.

"Then you're sure it's someone in town?"

Without turning he replied, "Almost positive, but I don't know who. I can't think of anyone in town who would be involved in cattle stealing."

There was silence in the room, and the low murmur of voices in the kitchen suggested that Orlena was telling her troubles to Mrs. O'Connor. "Well, I do wish you would forget the rustlers for a little while," Jenelle sighed. "You are home early tonight, the other two are busy, and I want you to myself."

Whirling from the window at Jenelle's wistful tones, Mr. Mavrich started across the room. There was a sudden splash, followed at once by Norman's groan and a merry peal of laughter from Jenelle, as the clatter of a pail tipping over and a stream of water spreading across the floor gave evidence that someone had forgotten to put away the pail of water after she had finished washing the windows. Ruefully Norman looked down at his boot, which was lying, still firmly wedged in the pail, in a pool of water, and felt the cold sensation of something wet soaking his sock. "I hope you are done washing windows, Jenelle," he remarked dryly, carefully making his way through the lake he had unintentionally created, to sit down and pull off his wet sock.

Jenelle, overcome with laughter, couldn't speak.

"Were you saying that the floor needed washing too?" Norman asked, wringing out his wet sock and gazing at the spreading water. His face was grave though his eyes twinkled, and Jenelle burst into another gale of laughter, which had the affect of bringing Mrs. O'Connor and Orlena to the door to find out the cause of the merriment.

Laughing almost as much as Jenelle, Orlena helped Mrs. O'Connor wipe up the water while Norman extracted his boot from the pail. Jenelle was of no help, for she laughed until she cried and the others laughed too. All troubles were forgotten for the evening and, even after everyone had retired to their rooms for the night, whirlwinds of chuckles still caught Jenelle unexpectedly, causing her husband to shake his head with a smile. He hadn't heard her laugh this much for a long time.

The weather was perfect as ladies gathered at the Triple Creek Ranch for the sewing bee. Every window in the front room, dining room and parlor had been opened wide to allow the fresh spring breeze to blow in, while the sun shone with all its brilliance from a cloudless sky. The rooms were full of busy hands and the air filled with lively talk. Social events, like a sewing bee, the annual Sunday School picnic, or an occasional barn raising, were highlights for the ranch wives. Such times brought together the ladies from far and near, for other than church meetings, the social life of most women from the ranches was very sparse. Those from town had more interaction with others, but an event like this was one which all delighted in.

Gathered in a small group in a corner of the dining room sat Orlena and the other girls from school. Even Elvira Ledford, in spite of her words the day before, had come with her mother and now sat in aloof silence with the others, listening to the chatter around them. Charity had arrived with Connie a little later, and Orlena had quickly made room for her. Though she hadn't felt up to coming, Mrs. Hearter had insisted her daughters attend without her.

The day passed quickly. Mrs. Greg, having accepted the offered ride from Connie, had been introduced and made welcome. Mrs. Ledford, on being questioned about her husband's health, had replied that he was no worse and even seemed slightly better. A few of the ladies from town mentioned the handsome young stranger who had just arrived from no one knew where, and it was circulated around the room that talk in town had it that he might be involved in the cattle rustling. Topics change often when there are many women gathered and the sewing bee was no exception. By the time the ladies began to gather their things and depart, Orlena was convinced that the only subjects not discussed were those she heard about every day in the school room.

As the last carriage and wagon drove down the lane, Jenelle sank into the rocking chair on the porch and gave a long sigh. "I hope there was as much work done today as there was talking. I was too busy to see what got finished."

Orlena sat down on the porch steps, cupping her chin in her hands. "I don't think Elvira came because she wanted to."

"Perhaps not." Jenelle's voice was soft. "But she did come. And you tried to make her feel welcome, didn't you?"

Orlena nodded.

"Then you'll have to leave the rest up to God. Keep trying and praying and God will do the rest." They sat in silence for some minutes before Orlena rose slowly and crossed the yard to the hen house.

On Sunday morning Jenelle was tired, too tired to drive into town for church, Norman decided, telling Mrs. O'Connor that he would remain at home with his wife. "If you would like to go, I'll have Lloyd drive you in."

Mrs. O'Connor accepted the offer with a smile, and Orlena begged to be allowed to go along. Her brother gave his consent readily.

To Mr. and Mrs. Mavrich the morning alone together was a delight. Things had been busy and there hadn't been much time to talk. They were almost sorry when the carriage pulled up and Mrs. O'Connor and Orlena returned.

It was late. The shining silvery light of the moon cast a soft, dreamlike glow over everything. The lights had been out all over the ranch for several hours when Norman was awakened by a whisper and a gentle shake.

"Norman!"

Jenelle's soft voice slowly penetrated his brain, and he stirred.

"Norman, who were you going to send for Dr.

French?"

"Hmm?" Turning his head, Norman opened one sleepy eye and then closed it again. It was too early to wake up, but just as he was about to slip back into slumber, he was shaken again and Jenelle's voice, more pleading than before, roused him.

"Norman, please! Who were you going to send?"

This time Norman opened both eyes and yawned. "What was that, Sweet?"

"Who were you going to send for Dr. French?"

"Oh, I don't know, whoever is around."

"Do you think he'll mind being awakened?"

"Who?" Norman was still half asleep and wondered faintly why Jenelle wasn't sleeping too.

"Whoever you decide to send!"

There was something in Jenelle's tones that had the effect of rousing Norman completely, for he sat up suddenly. "Jenelle, why are you asking these questions?"

"Because I . . . I think you had better send him soon."

CHAPTER 15

A NEW MAVRICH

"You mean—" Norman didn't wait for an answer but was already pulling on his clothes and shoving his feet into his boots. "I won't be gone long, Darling," he promised, pausing only long enough to kiss her quickly before hurrying from the room.

In less than five minutes Lloyd Hearter was on his way to the barn buttoning his shirt as he went.

Forgetting that his sister and Mrs. O'Connor were still sleeping, Norman took the stairs three at a time and dashed back to the bedroom.

"Norman," Jenelle's soft voice scolded from the pillow. "You'll wake the entire house with all your noise."

She was right, for moments later, after Norman had lit a lamp, a low knock sounded on their door. It was Mrs. O'Connor.

"Is everything all right?" she questioned anxiously. "Sure and it's an untimely hour for you to be racing around the house entirely if it isn't, Norman Mavrich." She shook her head, the lace on her white nightcap quivering as though it were alive.

"Mrs. O'Connor," a frightened voice sounded from the hall behind the housekeeper. "What is happening? I just saw someone ride off and I think it was Lloyd, and I heard someone running upstairs."

Norman gave a dismal groan while Jenelle couldn't keep back a faint laugh.

Briskly Mrs. O'Connor turned to Orlena. "It was only Norman sending someone for Dr. French. It's close to your sister's time and there is nothing you can do except go back to sleep."

Orlena didn't want to return to her room, and she certainly didn't feel like sleeping, but Mrs. O'Connor gave her no choice and almost pushed her back across the hall.

"Get some more sleep now. Tomorrow is a school day."

Once in her room again, Orlena stood for a moment looking at her bed. "I can't sleep." The thought of going to school tomorrow made her feel stubborn. "I just won't go," she told herself, crossing the room to curl up in her chair by the window with a blanket. "I'm sure to be needed here." She yawned. "I'll just wait here until Dr. French comes."

When the sun sent its first rays peeking above the horizon to see that things were ready for the coming day, they found Orlena sound asleep with her head on the windowsill. Downstairs Dr. French was sitting at the kitchen table with Norman.

"There is no reason you should remain in the house this morning," he was saying. "I'll call you when something happens. Sometimes little ones take their own precious time about getting here."

"What about Jenelle, Doc?"

"Your wife is doing just fine, Norman Mavrich. She's sleeping and that's what she should be doing right now, so you can either get some sleep yourself or get a bit of work done. I'll call you when something happens." He stood up.

Norman nodded but remained where he was. All thoughts of rustlers and coming round-ups were forgotten. All he could think of was his wife and their soon to be born baby.

When Orlena came down at last and discovered him, he

was still sitting at the table, but he looked up vaguely when she came in.

"How is Jenelle?"

"Sleeping. Are you ready for school?" he asked.

"Please don't make me go to school today," Orlena begged. "Please! I know I won't be able to do anything right and—oh, Norman, please say I can stay home!"

Realizing that she shared his anxiety, Norman nodded slowly. "All right—" he began.

"Oh, thank you, thank you, thank you!" Orlena threw her arms around her brother's neck and hugged him. "Now I'll go take care of the chickens," she said hurriedly, afraid that he might change his mind.

After his sister's departure from the kitchen, Norman rose with the realization that he still had a ranch to run and that even if he were to remain at the house, he should have a talk with Jim Hardrich about the work planned for the day. And Greg and Tompkins were supposed to be coming in for work this morning. The extra hands would be useful if he stayed behind.

It was a long morning for everyone at the ranch house. Norman hovered around the house and the bedroom until Dr. French ordered him in no uncertain terms to remain downstairs while Jenelle was sleeping. "There is nothing for you or anyone to do right now."

Orlena too was restless and several times half wished she were at school, while Norman regretted his decision to let her remain at home. At last Mack Davis, who had been left behind because of a slightly injured leg, took pity and, calling Orlena out to the corral where Lady and Beautiful Dreamer were, let her really get to know the young filly.

Pacing up and down the hall, Norman Mavrich clenched his hands and waited. There were sounds from the bedroom, and he listened with growing impatience for a certain sound. It came at last, the sound of a sharp slap and then a cry, the cry of a newborn baby. Suddenly halting where

he was, Norman sent up a swift but silent prayer of thanks.

A few minutes more and the door to the room opened, and Mrs. O'Connor beckoned him in.

"Jenelle!" Norman's eyes quickly sought those of his wife as he quietly slipped into the room and over to the bed where she lay, tired but with a new radiance on her face as she looked up at him. Stooping, he kissed her tenderly, and then his eyes shifted from his wife's shining eyes to the little bundle nestled in the crook of her am.

"It's a girl, Norman," Jenelle whispered.

Gently lifting the tiny bundle of babyhood in his strong hands, Norman gazed awestruck at the dark eyes over which long, dark lashes blinked, the light colored wisps of damp curls, the rosebud of a mouth, the tiny nose. This, this precious bit of flesh and blood was his daughter!

"She looks like you, Sweetheart," Norman breathed. Then he gently kissed the little newcomer while Jenelle watched with tired but starry eyes.

After a minute, Norman returned the baby to his wife's side and dropping to his knees, put an arm around both mother and daughter. They were alone in the room, Mrs. O'Connor and the doctor having slipped out after Norman entered.

"Are you happy?" Jenelle whispered.

"Happy? I don't think I could be any happier." And leaning closer, Norman's lips met hers in a long kiss.

Reluctantly standing up, Norman said softly, brushing his hand lightly over his wife's hair, "You get some rest now, Mama. I'll be back later." Gently he stroked the baby's cheek with one finger. "Precious little girl." His words were scarcely audible.

"Norman."

"Yes."

"Her name . . . Would you mind if we called her . . . Marian?"

Something in Norman's throat made it impossible for him to speak right then, so Jenelle's soft voice went on questioningly.

"Marian Rebekah?"

When he could command his voice again, it was somewhat husky. "For her two grandmothers waiting in heaven. Darling . . ." he couldn't go on, but pressing another kiss first on his wife's lips and then on his daughter's cheek, he turned and slipped from the room.

Pausing at the top of the stairs to gain control over his emotions, he whispered the name to himself. "Marian Rebekah Mavrich, welcome to the Triple Creek Ranch."

Orlena was ecstatic with delight when Norman told her she had a niece. "Oh, Norman! A baby girl! What is her name? Can I go see her now? What does she look like? Is Jenelle all right? What—"

"Hold it!" Norman held up his hand laughing. "First things first. Her name is Marian Rebekah and Jenelle is resting. You can see them both later."

"Marian Rebekah," Orlena mused. "Wasn't Marian—" She paused and looked up.

Norman nodded. "Yes, Marian was Mother's name. And Rebekah was Jenelle's mother's name."

Both brother and sister were silent for a full minute. Then, giving a sigh, Orlena burst out, "I wish I could run all the way to town and tell Charity! Oh, Norman, couldn't I go to school this afternoon?"

Chuckling, Norman shook his head. "How much work would you be able to do?"

"Nothing, I'm sure," his sister admitted. "But I want to tell someone! Oh, please, say I may!"

Glancing up at the sun, Norman hesitated. "If I let you go, you won't be able to see Jenelle or the baby until after school."

"Couldn't I just peek in at them before I leave?" Orlena asked, torn between her desire to stay and see this new baby which had come and had suddenly made her an aunt, and telling Charity and all the others at school the news. "And couldn't I make it before noon if I ride Anything?"

Right then Dr. French came out of the house with his hat on. "Mavrich, I'll be heading back to town. Your wife and daughter are both resting well, and I'll be back to see them later."

"Doc," Norman said quickly and hurried over to the doctor's buggy where he spoke for a few minutes in low tones. At the doctor's nod, he turned to Orlena and asked. "How quickly can you get ready, Sis?"

"I'll be down in five minutes!" And the girl flew into the house and up to her room.

When she came out of her room with her school dress on and her books in her arm, she paused, hesitated, and then, on tip-toe, crept across the hall. The door wasn't shut all the way and only a slight nudge pushed it wider. Cautiously peering in, Orlena saw her sister lying in the bed with no one else around.

Jenelle, hearing the soft creak of the floor, opened her eyes and smiled when she saw Orlena's face. "Come in, Orlena," she whispered, "and meet your niece."

With wide eyes, Orlena slipped across the room to the bedside and stared down at the bundle nestling beside Jenelle.

"Isn't she beautiful?" Jenelle asked.

Orlena had never seen a baby so young and small. In fact, she had scarcely seen any babies, for she had spent many years away at boarding schools, and her grandmother's friends never had babies around when they called or received visitors. Mutely she nodded.

The tiny bundle stirred and a little fist found its way out of the blanket.

Reaching down a hand, Orlena glanced at Jenelle, and receiving her nod, touched the little hand which opened and then grasped her finger with a tight baby hold.

"Marian Rebekah, this is your Aunt Orlena. I think she's going to school to tell everyone of your arrival."

Smiling a little guiltily at Jenelle's words, Orlena nodded. "I . . . I wasn't supposed to bother you—"

"You didn't," Jenelle assured. "I was hoping you would come up soon. Have a good day at school."

Orlena nodded, and with great reluctance gently pulled her finger free and hurried from the room.

As Norman assisted her into the carriage, he glanced at her face curiously, for a look of delighted wonder was on it which hadn't been there before. "I hope she didn't wake Jenelle," he thought, watching the buggy drive away.

Orlena had been right when she had told her brother she didn't think she'd be able to do anything in school. It took all of her concentration and strong will to pay attention at all and, if Miss Hearter hadn't been so understanding and refrained from asking her any direct question, she would have failed miserably. As soon as school was dismissed, Orlena turned to her seat-mate. "Charity, can't I go home with you and tell your mother about the baby?"

"Of course you can. Come on!" And Charity pulled her friend out of the school house. "Are you going to tell Mrs. Greg?"

Orlena nodded, too out of breath with excitement to talk.

Mrs. Hearter and Mrs. Greg were both pleased by the news Orlena brought and, though she would have liked to stay longer in town, Orlena knew she would have to hurry home so Norman wouldn't worry about her. Waving good-bye to Mrs. Greg and Charity, she started off.

As she was walking down the main street past the saloon, a few men staggered out and approached her. Drawing to one side, Orlena only glanced at them, for no one had ever bothered her before. But one of the men noticed her and came over until he stood before her.

"Well now, who've we got here?" he asked, and his breath reeked with liquor.

Starting back, Orlena, her face growing slightly pale, replied, "I'm Orlena Mavrich. Please let me pass."

"Mavrish is it?" chuckled the man as his companions

came up. "Look't here, boys, this here's a Mavrish."

The other two men laughed roughly and the first man reached out and jerked one of her curls. "Ain't you a purty thing."

"Ouch! Leave me alone!" Slapping his hand away, Orlena backed up a few steps, her eyes flashing though her face was pale.

"She's a feisty one, Boss," laughed one man moving to the side of the girl.

"Ya gonna let her get away with sassing you?" questioned the other.

CHAPTER 16

DREARY WEATHER

"Nope," grunted the first. "I've got ta teash them Mavrishes a lesson and I—"

Before another word could be said, a new voice, firm and cool, sounded. "Leave her alone."

"Well, if'n it ain't Mis'er Bruce. What's the kid ta you?" the first man asked sneeringly.

"She's a girl, and I won't stand for the mistreating of any womenfolk. Now leave her alone, all three of you." The words were even and the young man took a step closer.

"Ya goin' ta fight all three of us at once?" inquired the steadiest man.

"If I have to." The cool response seemed to irritate the first man and he reached out to pull Orlena's curls again, but his hand didn't ever reach her, for Mr. Bruce stepped in and with one well placed blow, had knocked the man to the street. "Are you going to leave now?" he asked of the other two men who were staring at him.

That one blow seemed to have knocked the fight out of all three troublemakers, for neither of the others made a move to take on the young stranger. The drunken man on the ground muttered something as his companions hauled him up and started down the road. Orlena could hear one of them remonstrating with the boss. "Come on, Blomberg, ya can't fight that man when yer drunk."

"Are you all right, Miss?"

Orlena turned from the retreating forms of her tormentors to the face of her rescuer. Nodding, she whispered, "Thank you."

Mr. Bruce winked quickly as he picked up her books, which she had dropped in her fright, and slipped something between them. "Here are your books, Miss. I don't think you'll have any more trouble with them," and he glanced down the street.

Still dazed by her experience, Orlena reached out for her books and started on her way again, turning to look back once or twice to see Mr. Bruce standing where she had left him. As long as he was watching, she felt safe, but on reaching the crossroad and turning towards the ranch, she began to run. Clutching her books close, her feet flew over the ground. She knew she had been late already when she had left the Gregory house, but now with the last delay—Would Norman be out looking for her? She half hoped he would each time she stopped to catch her breath and press her aching side.

As she turned down the lane leading onto the Triple Creek, she could see someone striding towards her. In another minute Norman was beside her.

"Why are you so late?" he asked. "Orlena, what is wrong?" He had noticed his sister's pale face. "What happened?"

Gulping air into her burning lungs, Orlena blurted, "I didn't know what they were going to do . . . He knocked one of them down . . . he was drunk . . . And Mr. Bruce left you a note, I think . . . I ran all the way and—" She sagged against him, her heart pounding and her legs trembling.

"Wait a minute, Sis, slow down. Who was in a fight and what did you mean about Mr. Bruce leaving me a note? No, on second thought, let's wait until we get into the house. You're shaking." With his arm around her, Norman silently walked back up the lane, up the steps, and into the house with Orlena. He had been about to saddle up a horse and go looking for her when Davis had spied her coming down the road.

"She's home, Mrs. O'Connor," Norman called softly up the stairs.

Mrs. O'Connor's face appeared at the top. "Thank God!" she whispered fervently.

Leading his sister into the front room, Norman placed her in a chair, brought her a glass of water, and then, drawing up his own chair, sat down and asked, "Now, what happened?"

After drawing a deep breath, Orlena began and her brother didn't interrupt her except once. "Do you know who the man was who started bothering you first?"

"I think one of his friends called him Blomberg."

The name brought a flash to Norman's grey eyes, but all he said was, "Go on."

When she had finished, Orlena found the piece of paper slipped in by Mr. Bruce and handed it to Norman.

Without a word, Norman opened and read the paper. "Some things are starting to make sense now," he muttered, his brows drawn together and his fingers tapping the paper. "I don't—" He stopped abruptly and looked at his sister. "Did you read this?"

She shook her head.

"Did anyone see you talking with Bruce besides those three men?"

Again she shook her head. "I don't think so. I didn't see anyone."

Norman was silent for so long after her reply that Orlena grew restless and asked, "May I go change now? Mrs. O'Connor will be expecting my help in the kitchen."

"What? Oh, yes, certainly. And you might look in on Jenelle and Baby while you are up there. She'll want to see that you're all right. But Orlena," he added as she reached the door. "Don't mention the last delay."

Nodding, Orlena slipped up to her room.

During the night a spring storm came up, and by morning the creeks were flooded and the road into town was a solid mass of mud. The rain was still coming down steadily when Orlena made her way down to the breakfast table the following morning. In the dining room she found her brother staring out the window.

"Good morning," she greeted him.

He returned the greeting in an absent manner.

Wandering into the kitchen, Orlena leaned against the table and addressed Mrs. O'Connor. "It's not the same down here without Jenelle. And Norman hasn't spoken much since I returned home yesterday." She sighed dismally. "I think I'll be glad to go to school today."

"Sure and you won't be going to school today," Mrs. O'Connor said quietly. "Your brother told me that first thing. He's been out to the barn doing chores and said the roads are nothing but mud entirely."

With a dismal groan, Orlena sank down onto a chair, her shoulders slumped. "What am I going to do? Norman," she turned to her brother as he entered the kitchen, "can't I go to school?"

Norman shook his head. "No. The roads are almost impassable already and this rain doesn't show much sign of letting up any time soon. Sorry, Sis, but you'll have to remain at home." He smiled sympathetically down at her before crossing the room to open the door and look out.

A frown came over Orlena's face and she sighed loudly. "I won't have anything to do today," she whined. "Please, Norman, can't you take me?"

Norman was tired. He had been up late the night before talking over some plans with his foreman and now was worried about his men who were out on patrol among the cattle. He was thankful Jenelle and Baby Marian Rebekah were doing well so he didn't have to worry about them much. He knew Mrs. O'Connor would see to it that Jenelle got the rest she needed.

"Please take me, Norman!"

"No, Orlena," his voice was more stern then he meant it to be. "There is no way a wagon or carriage could make it to town. The mud would be up to your ankles. You'll just have to find something to do at home."

"Are you going out to ride?" she asked.

"I'll probably have to later."

"Then I don't see why you couldn't take me to school." It wasn't often now that Orlena let her temper or selfish nature get the better of her, but as so often happens even to stronger Christians, she had neglected to read her Bible yesterday in all the worry over Jenelle in the morning, and by evening hadn't felt like reading so, after a hurried prayer, which was more lip service than actual prayer, she had gone to bed. When she awoke to the sound of rain, and saw how dismal and dreary everything was, her mood didn't improve. She had been thinking of how she would tell Charity and some of the other girls at school of her rescue by the stranger in town and had imagined what they would say. Now her dreams were shattered, and she felt that it wasn't fair.

Turning from the doorway, Norman said quietly, "Orlena, you are not going to school today. That's final. I strongly doubt more than half a dozen students will be able to make it in this weather anyway."

Orlena knew better than to plead any longer, but she sat with her arms folded and a pout on her face.

"Come now and sit down, Norman," Mrs. O'Connor directed briskly. "Breakfast is ready."

The meal was eaten in strained silence save for the rain and an occasional rumble of thunder. Norman, though it was hard at times, had learned through much experience that man may plan his ways but the Lord directs his steps. Often Norman's plans had had to be laid aside because of weather or other circumstances beyond his control. It wasn't always easy, but today seemed especially difficult.

Excusing himself from the table as soon as he was finished, Norman hurried upstairs to his room to check on Jenelle. He found her awake, Marian in her arms.

Sitting down on the bed beside her, Norman looked down at his little daughter. "How are you this morning, Jenelle?"

With a soft laugh, Jenelle replied, "I'm doing just fine and so is little Marian. How is Orlena getting to school with this rain?"

"She's not. The roads are ankle deep in mud and there's no sign of the rain letting up." As the baby began to whimper, he took her in his arms and his voice softened. "If I didn't have things to do, I'd like nothing better than to remain right here today, with you and your mother, Marian."

With a yawn, Marian stretched and opened her dark eyes.

"Good morning, Little One. What do you think of all this rain, huh? Just be glad you don't have any place to go in it. Yes, you can stay right here with your mama without a care in the world."

Lying among the pillows, Jenelle smiled as she listened to her husband talk to their daughter and watched his strong, sure hands gently holding her.

"Now, sweet thing, your papa has to go out in the rain and have a talk with Mr. Hardrich and the men. Don't worry though," he added, as Marian squirmed a little and began to fuss, "I'll be careful. Now you be a good girl for Mama."

A tender kiss was placed on the tiny nose and Norman handed the baby back to his wife.

"Do you really have to go out in this, Norman?"

He nodded. "Yes. But don't fret. Though I don't think the rain is going to quit, it has let up some. You rest today, Sweetheart, and I'll be back as soon as I can." A quick kiss and then he was gone.

As Norman was putting on his slicker, Orlena came into the kitchen. "Norman, where are you going?" she exclaimed.

"I have to go talk to Hardrich," Norman explained, reaching for his hat.

"That's not fair! You get to go out and do something, and I'm stuck here in the house. I should have stayed in bed this morning!"

"Then go back to bed, if you wish, no one is stopping you." Norman spoke in a matter of fact tone, but it only served to irritate his young sister further.

She stamped her foot. "You don't care if I have anything to do or not," she snapped. "If I—" she stopped suddenly as her brother turned around and looked at her.

Drawing out a chair, he nodded to it. "Sit." Then, dropping his hat on the table, Norman pulled out another chair and sat down. For several minutes he didn't speak but toyed with a button on his jacket. "What is wrong, Orlena?" he asked at last, his voice showing concern.

Faced with the question aloud, Orlena shook her head. "I don't know!" Her lips trembled and she tried to blink back her tears.

"Are you really upset because of school, or is there another reason?" he pressed.

"I don't know."

"Then I think it's time we find out. Orlena, did you have plans for today and are upset that they had to be changed?"

Orlena shrugged, her eyes on her hands twisting themselves in her skirt. She didn't want to admit her reason for wanting to go to school. What would Norman think of her?

"Did you spend time with your Savior this morning, asking for His guidance?" When no answer came, Norman reached over and lifted her chin with his finger. "Orlena, how can you expect help for the day if you don't ask for it? How can you start your day without your Heavenly Father and expect it to run smoothly? Did you even pick up your Bible this morning?"

A very faint shake of the head and Orlena turned her face away. She hated to admit it now, but she had been so busy thinking about what the others would say to her story that she hadn't once thought of the Book which had helped her before.

As the minutes slowly passed and Orlena still didn't speak, Norman asked softly, "Do you want to continue your day on your own?"

"No." The words, scarcely above a whisper, were followed by a quivering sigh.

Norman stood up. "Then why don't you go to Jesus and tell Him everything, and ask for forgiveness for ignoring Him, and ask for help."

Raising her eyes and meeting the grey ones looking down at her, she nodded, rose, and was turning away when Norman pulled her back and hugged her.

"If I didn't have work to do, Sis, I'd stay and—"

"That's all right," Orlena sniffed, smiling, though her eyes were wet with tears. "I'll find something to do." And she turned and hurried from the room, afraid that she would start to cry before she reached her room. All she wanted then was to make things right with her Savior.

CHAPTER 17

TWISTED FENCES

It wasn't raining as hard as it had been earlier when Norman stepped off the porch and headed towards the bunkhouse. The wind still blew in gusts, but the sky had lightened. The ground, saturated as it was, oozed and sucked at his boots with each step he took. "It would be a nightmare trying to ride on a road through this stuff," he muttered, moving to the grass beside muddy path. There it was a little easier to walk, though parts of the grass looked like ponds or swamps. Pausing on the porch of the bunkhouse, Norman stood for a moment looking off in the direction of the range. Where were the men out there? Were they all right? He wished he knew.

Opening the door, Mr. Mavrich stepped inside and took off his dripping jacket.

The men looked up, somewhat startled. "Mavrich," Hardrich asked, "is something wrong?"

After hanging up his hat, he shook his head. "Not what you're thinking. It's just that this rain has brought a change of plans. And," he added, "I'm a bit concerned about Burns, Maynard, Alden, Tracy and Wilson. The creeks are all bound to be flooded and . . ."

"They'll have taken shelter in one of the line shacks, sir," Lloyd said.

"That's what has me worried, Hearter," Mr. Mavrich

replied, resting his hands on the back of a straight-backed chair. "There are two or three which never got repaired in the fall. One of them is right near Penny Creek, and if the creek floods, well, it might not be there any more."

"Tracy and Burns know that shack isn't safe," Scott put in. "I heard Tracy mention something about it when we rode past it a few days ago. I don't think either of them would take shelter there."

"What about the others?"

No one answered.

"If this rain would let up . . ." Norman began tapping his fingers slowly on the chair. "Of course, we could ride even in the rain, but . . ."

The men were silent, waiting for their boss to finish his thinking. They trusted his judgment and, if he said they were to ride, not one of them would hesitate to obey. His concern for the other men also added to the respect they all felt for him.

"Hardrich," Mr. Mavrich said at last, "I'm going to take Scott, Barker and Hearter. We'll ride out and check on the men. I don't think we should wait until the rain stops because I don't think it's going to stop any time soon."

Hardrich nodded. "Right, sir."

"St. John, make sure you've got some hot food ready whenever we get back because I think it'll be wanted. Davis, take it easy with that leg. I want you ready for the saddle when the rain does stop and things dry up a bit."

The older man nodded with a grin.

"All right, men, you ready?" Norman Mavrich turned to the three men he had named who had been quickly preparing for their ride as he spoke with the others.

"Yes, sir!" came the answer as the men snatched up their hats.

"Then let's go!"

A distant rumble of thunder sounded as the door of the bunkhouse was opened and the men set out through the mud and water for the barn. Quickly the horses were saddled, and

Norman issued orders rapidly as they worked.

"When we get to Penny Creek, Scott and Barker, I want the two of you to head along the northern area. Check the line shacks, and if you find the men, fire two quick shots in the air, wait a moment and fire two more, and then stay there unless the shack isn't safe. Hearter, you stick with me, and we'll take the south line."

"What if we don't find the men?" Barker asked, swinging up on his horse. "You want us to keep going?"

"Yes. If you don't find them or hear signal shots from us, keep going and circle around by Outlook Point, but stay out of Deadlock Canyon. With all this rain we've been having it could be flooded, and there's danger of a flash flood if the hills have been getting as much of this storm as we have, especially if that old beaver dam breaks. Stick to high ground as much as possible. Now let's go!" Norman had mounted Captain as he finished his instruction, and now led the way out of the barn.

No fast riding could be done with all the mud, but, sticking to the grassy areas and highest ground, the four men made better time than Mr. Mavrich had thought possible. With collars turned up on their slickers and hats pulled low to keep as much of the rain off as they could, the four men rode steadily for over an hour before coming to the crest of a ridge.

Pulling up their horses, they gazed before and below them.

Barker let out a whistle and shook his head. "That creek sure is flooded, Mr. Mavrich!"

Norman only nodded as his eyes searched for the best place to cross. It was difficult to tell where the creek bed was for the water had spread out several feet from its bank on both sides.

"Look!" Lloyd's shout caused the others to turn their gaze and follow the direction he was pointing. "Isn't that what used to be one of the line shacks?"

"That's what I was afraid of," Mr. Mavrich said grimly.

Standing halfway in the flooded area was the remains of the shack. Much of the roof had caved in, and from the way the whole place sagged, those watching wouldn't have been surprised to see it collapse at any time into the muddy waters of Penny Creek.

The sight of the half destroyed line shack urged the men into action, for they wondered where their companions were and what condition the other shacks were in. Riding slowly down the slippery hillside, Norman urged his horse carefully into the flooded waters of Penny Creek. The others followed.

Part way through, Captain hesitated. "Come on, Captain," Norman urged softly. "I'll let you have your head if you want it, but we've got to get across. I know you'd rather walk on land you can see, but this is the best we've got until we reach the other side. Come on now." With his gentle talk, Norman succeeded in starting his horse onward again. Slowly, step by careful step, the men moved forward. Suddenly Captain sank, and Norman felt water pour into his boots.

"We've entered the creek!" Mr. Mavrich called back to the other men. It only took a minute for the ranch horse to regain his footing and soon he was scrambling up the other bank.

At last safely across the flooded stream, the four men looked at each other. "If Penny Creek is this full, I'd hate to see what Crystal Creek looks like," Scott remarked, dumping water out of his boots.

The others nodded, emptying boots and looking back at the way they had come.

"Let's ride."

With Lloyd beside him, Norman started out towards the south line while Barker and Scott headed the other way. The rain had turned into a mere drizzle and Norman glanced up at the sky. How he wished the clouds would break and let the sun come out!

After riding for five minutes together, Mr. Mavrich turned to his young hand beside him. "Let's spread out. We'll cover more ground that way. Stay within sight, if possible, or within sound at least."

"Yes, sir!" And Hearter nudged Spitfire away from Captain and off to the right.

Though several groups of cattle were found, bunched together as cattle will during storms, there was no sign of any cattlemen. With all the rain, any tracks the shod horses would have made had been washed out. No sound of signal shots were heard either. Steadily the two riders moved onward. Norman hoped this meant that the men had taken shelter in one of the sturdier line shacks and were waiting out the storm, but he couldn't quite rid himself of a feeling he'd had all morning that something wasn't quite right.

"Hearter!" he called.

"Sir?"

"There's a shack just over the next rise. It's the only one our way. We'll head for it."

The young man nodded and turned his horse's head in that direction. He was also hoping that they would either find the men or hear shots from Barker and Scott. "Mr. Mavrich, do you think we'll actually be able to hear signal shots from Scott and Barker?"

"I don't know. It might depend on if it's raining and where we are."

Neither man spoke again until Lloyd suddenly exclaimed, "Mr. Mavrich, do you smell smoke?"

Quickly scanning the distant sky, Norman thought he could just make out a faint line of smoke. "Come on!"

Urging their tired mounts to a faster pace, the men hurried on. After finding more solid ground in a rocky area, the horses made better time than they had plodding through the muck and mire.

"Look! The shack!" Norman pointed to a distant building where a light glowed from the one window. Drawing his rifle, because it was louder than his handgun, Norman fired off two quick shots into the air, waited a moment and then fired two more. "Let's pray Scott and Barker heard those," Norman said, slipping his gun back into the scabbard on his saddle.

It was obvious that whoever was in the cabin had heard the shots also, for a new light showed where a door had been opened. Lloyd's shout was returned, and he waved his hat.

"I think at least two of the men are there, sir," Lloyd grinned.

"Let's hope they all are," Norman replied quietly.

Their hopes were realized when at last they reined in before the small shack and dismounted. Alden stood in the doorway and, in answer to his boss's anxious question, replied, "All five of us are here, sir."

Norman couldn't keep back a sigh of relief at the news.

"Let me take your horses," Maynard said, coming around the side of the house and holding out his hands for the reins. "I'll put them with the others."

There was something about the quiet way both men talked that made Norman ask quickly, "What's wrong, Alden?"

Alden didn't reply but stepped aside to allow his boss and Lloyd to enter the room.

The warm glow of a fire and a lit lantern hanging from the rafters filled the room with light, and Norman's eyes instantly fell on Tracy sitting on the floor near a figure lying under a blanket.

"What happened?" The words were sharp as Mr. Mavrich crossed the room in a few strides and dropped down beside the blanket which stirred.

"I'm all right, Boss," a voice said. It was Burns.

Swiftly drawing back the blanket, Norman saw the cut and bruised face of Burns, noticed his bandaged hand and the torn and dirty clothes. "What happened?" he asked again.

"Horse threw me," Burns coughed. "But the fences are down 'bout half a mile from here, Boss. We got ta get it fixed." He coughed again and struggled to sit up.

"Just lie still, Burns, while I take a look at you," Mr. Mavrich ordered firmly.

"Mr. Mavrich."

Norman turned his head briefly, and Tracy continued, "I found his horse wandering alone about one o'clock this morning, not long after the storm hit. It was almost three-thirty before Wilson and I found him and got him back here, where we found Maynard and Alden. He'd been thrown, and when we found him, he was trying to fix that fence in the pouring rain. He's been coughing since we first found him."

"How much of the fence is down?" Norman had been examining his ranch hand and was relieved to find no visible serious damage.

"A good five yards at least," Wilson answered. "There must have been a run off of water there because the posts were just lying on their sides and the wires were twisted and—" He shook his head.

Taking advantage of Norman's attention to someone besides himself, Burns pushed himself up and stated emphatically, "It wasn't water that washed them posts down!" He coughed and shook his head as Norman tried to gently push him back. "Let me finish."

Hearter stepped over, handing a canteen to Mr. Mavrich.

"Here, Burns, take a drink, and then I'll listen to you." Norman held out the canteen of water and the injured man took it and drank eagerly.

"I saw them pulling the posts down, and they cut some of the wires, but when I got there they rode off."

"Who did this?"

"Rustlers, sir." Leaning against the wall, Burns looked pleadingly at his boss. He had noticed the glances exchanged between his fellow cowboys and insisted, "It's true. And they're plannin' on bringin' more cattle in soon. Said everyone'd think—" A slight cough broke into his sentence and he raised a hand to his aching head, wincing as he touched a cut on his face.

Before Mavrich could say anything, Maynard entered the shack.

"Any sign of Scott and Barker?"

"No, sir. Perhaps they holed up in another shack. How are you feeling, Burns?"

The injured man nodded silently.

"Wilson, Tracy, you saw the fence down? Did you take time to examine it?" Norman looked from one man to the other.

"No, sir," Tracy said quickly. "Our thought was to get Burns and get in out of the storm. And none of us has been back there since."

Mr. Mavrich turned to Burns once more. "Are you sure you saw someone pulling down the fence?"

"Positive, sir! There were at least three of them or I would have tried to bring them in. I might've tried anyway, but I didn't have my ropes to tie 'em up with."

Nodding slowly, Mr. Mavrich pressed Burns' arm lightly and turned to the others. "We'll give our horses a fifteen minute rest and then, Maynard and Alden, you'll join Hearter and me and we'll head for that fence and take a look."

"I'll go along and show you where it is, sir," Burns offered, trying to stifle a cough and pushing back the blanket.

CHAPTER 18

MYSTERIOUS RIDERS

"Huh," grunted Mr. Mavrich, firmly holding the blanket where it was. "You're not going anywhere just yet, Burns. Right in this blanket you are going to stay, and I want you to rest. I'm leaving Tracy and Wilson to see to it that you do. Now," he said, turning to Tracy and Wilson as Burns sank back down and closed his eyes, "can you draw me a map of where the fence was down?"

For a few minutes the men bent their heads over the makeshift map and talked in low tones. At last Mr. Mavrich stood up, folded the paper and tucked it in his pocket.

"All right men, let's get the horses and head out. Wilson, if Scott and Barker arrive, you head out and bring me word. Tracy, you stay here and see if you can keep this cousin of yours resting."

"I'll try, sir," Tracy promised with a slight smile, watching the other men preparing to leave the small shack.

Wilson and Tracy's directions proved accurate and before long the fence line could be seen. And so could almost half a dozen head of cattle. Quickly Norman held up his hand and the men halted beside him.

"Whew!" Alden whistled softly. "What do you make of that, Mr. Mavrich?"

"I reckon Burns knew what he was talking about, after

all," Maynard remarked.

"Can any of you see the brands on them from here?" Norman questioned.

The answer was negative and Maynard offered to ride down and check them.

"All right—no, hold it! Look over there on that ridge." Norman pointed to a low hill not a great distance from the downed fence line but far enough away that it was beyond rifle shot. Nearing the crest of the hill, riding away from the Triple Creek, were the forms of three men on horseback.

"What would three riders be doing out in this weather heading away from that fence?" Lloyd asked.

"I can't think of anything good," Alden replied.

Once the distant riders had disappeared, Norman led the way down to the cattle. He had his suspicions and when he saw the brand on the cattle, he knew he had been right. The cattle were all Lucky Shoe stock.

"This has gone far enough!" he declared firmly, scanning the area, his eyes lingering longest at the place the riders had last been seen.

"You want us to follow them, sir?" Lloyd asked, eagerly. "There are more of us than of them."

But Mr. Mavrich shook his head. "We don't know how many are behind that hill. Besides, all this mud is tiring for the horses. But I think I may have a plan. Maynard, you're the best tracker we've got here. Look around and see if you can find signs of any horses having been near that fence. The rain will have washed out any signs of Tracy and Wilson's mounts. I want proof that they," and he nodded towards the hill, "weren't just some of Carmond's men out checking cattle."

Quickly Maynard dismounted, handing the reins to Lloyd, and moved over to take a look. Also swinging from his horse, Norman moved slowly among the cattle, looking them over carefully.

"These cattle have been traveling today, I'm guessing. How far, I can't say, but they are restless. Alden, did you notice any of Triple Creek's cattle grazing anywhere around

here?" Norman looked up as he came out of the small herd.

Tipping his head in thought, Alden hesitated. "No, I can't remember any being around here for several days. Do you think they were stolen? I know that fence wasn't down until last night, sir!"

"If cattle were stolen, I don't think it was here. At least not recently." Turning, Norman watched Maynard a few minutes before calling, "Find anything yet?"

Without raising his head, the cowhand replied, "Yep. There are plenty of tracks around here. Someone certainly drove those cattle across. I'd say more than one someone too. My guess is those three riders we saw had a good bit to do with this." He looked up. "Want me to see if I can follow the horses' tracks a ways?"

"Yes. Hearter, go with him. But," he added firmly, "don't either one of you get the idea of going farther than the bottom of that rise. There's no telling who or what is over it, and I can't spare any hands this time of year."

"Right, sir!" There was no hiding the excitement in Hearter's eyes as he rode off on Spitfire taking Maynard's horse along.

"Are we going to work on that fence, Mr. Mavrich?" Alden asked.

Norman nodded and soon both men were at work. Though the ground was muddy, and it was difficult digging new holes for the posts, by the time Maynard and Hearter returned with the assurance that the riders were most likely the ones responsible for the downed fence and driving the Lucky Spur cattle through, they had made fair progress. After stopping for a quick bite, for it was well past noon, all four men went back to work. Before they had finished, Wilson rode up with the news that Scott and Barker had made it to the shack and were resting their horses.

"Looks like the weather might clear before long, Mr. Mavrich," Wilson remarked, lending a hand at stretching the wire.

Norman grunted. "Good. If we're going to catch those

rustlers, we need some drier ground."

At last the fence was upright again, and Mr. Mavrich rode back to the shack with his men.

"Do you think they'll try anything else tonight?" Scott asked as the men sat around enjoying the warmth and dryness of the little shack.

Cupping his hand around his tin cup of coffee, Mr. Mavrich shook his head. "Hard telling. They may decide to lay low for a few days, or they may hope that we'll think that and try something else tonight." The room fell silent as the men waited for their boss to give his orders.

"I'm going to go on the assumption that they won't try anything else tonight. With all the rain and the flooding, it'd be awfully hard to move cattle very far and if we don't get more rain, they'd run the risk of leaving a good trail for us to follow.

"That means we're all heading back. Get your horses ready to go. Scott, see to Captain, and Hearter, get Comet ready. Burns," Mr. Mavrich turned to his injured hand, "you're staying inside until we're ready to go."

Rapidly the men left to follow orders, leaving Mr. Mavrich to put out the fire and generally put the shack to rights.

In less than ten minutes the men were all in the saddle and riding towards home. The sun was beginning to peek through the dark clouds and the horses seemed to have less trouble with mud. Penny Creek was higher than before and the men followed it downstream until they came to a better place to cross.

Meanwhile, back at the ranch house, Orlena, having spent time reading her Bible and on her knees really praying, went soberly down to the kitchen. She knew her Heavenly Father had forgiven her for her neglect and the complaining words and actions of that morning, but she also knew she should apologize to Mrs. O'Connor. Rarely had Orlena apologized to anyone and it was difficult to do so now. For several minutes she stood in the dining room wishing she could get out of it. Twice she turned and started towards the stairs, but each time she was stopped by the prick of her conscience which whispered, "You know you were wrong. Putting it off won't make it right."

At last, with a desperate effort to get it done, she hurried into the kitchen and blurted out, "Mrs. O'Connor, I'm sorry for being so complaining this morning. Will you forgive me?"

Silence was the only answer.

Startled, Orlena looked around to discover that Mrs. O'Connor wasn't even in the kitchen. Giving a half-embarrassed little laugh, Orlena turned and saw the housekeeper bustling down the stairs towards the kitchen, tying on an apron as she came.

Without giving Mrs. O'Connor a chance to speak, Orlena repeated her apology and then waited.

"Forgive you, child? To be sure I will. Now, if you've nothing better to do, suppose you help me bake a pie for supper."

Orlena had never spent much time in the kitchen, except when she was washing dishes, for she was usually in school or busy elsewhere when the meals were made, and she had never learned any culinary arts at Madam Viscount's Seminary! Mrs. O'Connor was a careful and thorough teacher and enjoyed sharing her skills with the once spoiled and haughty tyrant of Mrs. Marshall Mavrich's house.

To her surprise, Orlena found that there was something satisfying in mixing and measuring ingredients and watching them evolve into a recognizable dish. As she carefully slid the pie into the oven and shut the door, she exclaimed, "I never knew what was in a pie before! Do you think it will be any good?"

"To be sure and why wouldn't it be?"

Orlena frowned. "I don't know, but . . . I hope it tastes good. Mrs. O'Connor, will you teach me how to bake more things?"

"I will indeed," Mrs. O'Connor promised with a smile. "Now tis best if we wash up these dishes while the pie bakes. Then we will get dinner."

Orlena was surprised to find the morning had gone by so quickly.

After dinner was eaten and cleared away, Orlena slipped upstairs and tapped lightly on her sister's door. On hearing a soft summons to enter, she opened the door and looked in. "Are you too tired for company?" she asked.

"Of course not," Jenelle smiled. "Marian and I have been sleeping most of the morning and are ready for a visit. Aren't we, Sweetheart?" Jenelle glanced down with loving eyes at the little face so innocent and perfect. Looking up again she said, "Pull up my rocker and talk to me. I want to hear all about the morning. Would you like to hold Marian?" she added as Orlena settled herself in the rocking chair next to the bed.

"I might break her."

Jenelle laughed softly. "Babies don't break that easily. Here." Sitting up, Jenelle lifted her baby and placed her in Orlena's arms. "That's right," she praised. "You are doing just fine."

Speechless, Orlena gazed down at the tiny face of her niece. She scarcely dared to move for fear of dropping or in some way harming the infant. She was so little! When Marian stretched, Orlena lifted frightened eyes to Jenelle. She didn't know what to do.

"Would you like me to take her now?"

Orlena nodded quickly and soon Marian was snuggling in the bed beside her mother once again.

For several minutes Jenelle lay watching her young sister's face. It was very expressive, she realized, noticing the slight smile disappear into a sober look, and the grey eyes, so like those of Norman, seemed to fill for they blinked quickly a few times and Orlena swallowed hard. "Tell me about it, Orlena," Jenelle said softly.

"I . . . I was awful this morning!" she blurted out quickly, somehow sensing that Jenelle was genuinely interested. "I wanted to go to school and when Norman said I couldn't go, I got upset and didn't talk very nicely. It wasn't that I really wanted to go to school. I wanted to see Charity and—" she stopped and drew up her knees to rest her chin on them. Norman had told her not to tell Jenelle why she was really late yesterday, but that was then. Could she tell her now?

"And you wanted to tell her about Blomberg stopping you?"

The softly spoken words startled Orlena, and she nodded. How had Jenelle learned about it?

"Norman told me," was the answer to the unasked question. "And then what?"

Hugging her knees, Orlena resumed her tale. "I got upset and argued and complained. I know I didn't read my Bible like I should have this morning, but was it wrong to want to tell Charity about yesterday?"

Jenelle was silent for a minute, praying for wisdom to help this young Christian walk in the right path. "That depends on several things. Was the reason you wanted to tell her simply because you want to tell her everything that happens? Did you want her to know so that she would be extra careful walking around town? Or did you want her and possibly others to hear about it and think of you in a more 'glorified manner' so to speak, because you were 'rescued by a handsome stranger from some drunken scoundrels'?"

As Jenelle finished her last question, Orlena's cheeks flushed, and she kept her eyes on the opposite wall. The silence deepened, and Orlena fidgeted; first putting her right leg down, then her left, she twisted in her seat, rocked a few times, crossed her arms, then tucked her feet up and settled herself once again. All this time Jenelle waited patiently.

Finally, not meeting Jenelle's quiet blue eyes, Orlena admitted, "Because I wanted them to think I was more interesting."

"Do you think that was a good reason for telling the story? Orlena, dear, it is easy to want people to think better of us or to think that we live a more exciting life or have finer things, that's in our human nature. But it isn't what Christ wants. If we want to live for Him, we must put Him first. Do you think your motives would have changed if you had spent time in His Word and in prayer this morning before going down?"

Remembering the verse she had read after her brother had left, about no man thinking of himself more highly then he ought, she nodded. "But it was exciting," she protested, looking at Jenelle for the first time since the conversation started.

Jenelle laughed a little but cringed as well. "Did you think that when it was happening?"

Wrapping her arms around her knees again, Orlena thought. "I was mad at first and then I guess I was scared, until Mr. Bruce came. Then I was afraid he would get hurt. But, Jenelle, you should have seen him knock that one man down! I like Mr. Bruce."

CHAPTER 19

A GAMBLE

"Why doesn't Norman hire him to work on the ranch? Couldn't he find things for him to do? I think he should get married and live around here."

With a shake of her head and a smile, Jenelle chided gently, "Don't go trying to play matchmaker at your age, Orlena. Mr. Bruce may not like it around here for long. He agreed to do some work and then he may move on. Perhaps he doesn't want to settle down again. He's traveled quite a bit and says he hasn't found any place he has wanted to settle. You know he only came by to see your brother since they went to school together. He may stay around and help with the spring round-up if Norman asks, or he could just ride on."

It was obvious that Orlena hadn't heard much of what Jenelle said for she stared dreamily out the open window and remarked, "Mrs. Connie Bruce would sound well."

"Orlena Mavrich!" Jenelle exclaimed. "Don't mention that to anyone!"

Shocked by her usually quiet sister's tones, Orlena looked startled. "I . . . I . . . I wasn't going to," she stammered. "The thought just came to me."

Jenelle softened her voice. "I know you didn't mean anything, but, Dear, playing matchmaker is not a game. Marriage is a very special thing, and think of how Miss

Hearter would feel if you mentioned something to Charity and she told her sister. Do you think Miss Hearter would feel comfortable around Mr. Bruce if they should chance to meet?"

Orlena shook her head soberly. "I won't say anything to anyone," she promised. "But, Jenelle," she added shyly, though her eyes began to twinkle, "don't you think it would be nice if they did meet and like each other?"

It was impossible for Jenelle to keep a straight face. "I hadn't even thought of it until now, but—" she smiled. "Let's change the subject."

Giggling, Orlena was happy to oblige and told about her experience at pie making with Mrs. O'Connor and how she was going to help prepare supper.

As Mr. Mavrich and his men arrived back in the yards, they were welcomed by St. John, Davis and Jim Hardrich. The latter didn't ask any questions as they rode up, but sent St. John into the bunkhouse to prepare to serve the men a hot supper as soon as they came in. Norman dismounted near the bunkhouse and, handing his reins to Lloyd, told Davis to inform Mrs. O'Connor that he'd be along shortly. "Tracy, take Burns' horse."

Burns protested. "I can manage, Mr. Mavrich. The ground was soft when I landed."

Grunting significantly, Triple Creek's boss raised an eyebrow and tipped his head in the direction of the bunkhouse. No words were necessary. Slowly Burns dismounted, coughing, and Norman walked beside him into the dry house. Though no doctor, Norman had acquired a practical knowledge of the most common ailments to be found on a ranch, as most ranch bosses or foremen had, and was quite adept at handling most slight sicknesses or injuries.

When the men came in from the barn, having taken care of their horses, Norman was putting on his hat and preparing to head to the house. "Hardrich," he waylaid his foreman, "I'll be back later to talk over some new plans. What we've discovered today sheds new light on things and I may have a way to catch these gallyhoos."

"Don't hurry." And Hardrich grinned at his young boss's new name for the rustlers. "I'm not going anywhere."

Orlena had been watching somewhat impatiently out the window since Mr. Davis had delivered Norman's message. Would he never come? When she at last saw him leave the bunkhouse, she flew to the door and flinging it open, called, "Norman, supper is ready! Hurry!"

Quickening his pace, Norman was soon in the kitchen, taking off his jacket and hanging up his hat. He begged to be allowed to change from his damp clothes before sitting down to supper, and reluctantly Orlena consented, though she called after him, "Jenelle won't tell you anything about supper!"

This call filled Norman with curiosity and, in spite of his sister's positive statement, he tried to question Jenelle about its meaning.

But Jenelle ignored his questions, asking instead if things had gone well and were the men all right and had he brought them all back or were some remaining out on the range tonight. As Norman kissed her before going down to his supper, she whispered, "Enjoy it, Darling. I've already eaten."

Still puzzled, but quite hungry, Norman hurried down to the dining room where Mrs. O'Connor and Orlena were waiting.

After asking the blessing, Norman remarked, "This looks and smells good, Mrs. O'Connor, and I'm mighty hungry. Didn't have time for much dinner today." Lifting his fork, he suddenly became aware that Orlena was watching his every move closely and, though she tried not to appear to be doing so, Mrs. O'Connor was also observing him. He glanced down. Yes, his shirt was buttoned right, he didn't notice any dirt on his hands and he wasn't using his left hand for his fork. What could they be interested in? Although still slightly puzzled, Norman's hunger overcame his wonder, and he began to eat heartily.

After the first few mouthfuls of each thing, the meat, the biscuits, the potatoes, Orlena would exchange glances with Mrs. O'Connor, who in turn would nod and smile. When he was half way through with his second helpings of everything, Norman asked, "All right, what's going on? You two look like you've been into mischief of some sort."

Orlena's face grew pink, and she exclaimed quickly, "There's pie for dessert!"

"Oh?" Norman's tone and the look he bestowed on his sister brought on a few giggles from her. "Am I supposed to guess what's going on, or are you going to tell me?"

It was Mrs. O'Connor who replied. "Finish your supper, Norman, and then Orlena will serve the pie since Jenelle isn't here to do it."

Seeing that he wasn't going to get anything out of them, Norman returned to his meal, his mind playing back the events of the day, as well as his half formed plans for catching the rustlers. He would have to get the assistance of several extra people, but he thought it would work. If there was no more rain during the night, he'd ride into town in the morning with Orlena and have a talk with the sheriff and get his help. Perhaps while he was in town, he'd also get a chance to speak with Bruce, though that might ruin any other chance he had of getting inside information. As he was thinking, Norman absentmindedly nodded when Orlena asked if he was ready for a piece of pie. It wasn't until the plate in front of him was changed that he returned his thoughts to the present.

"This looks wonderful, Mrs. O'Connor," he said, forking a bite into his mouth. "And it tastes as good as it looks."

"You really like it?" Orlena asked. She had been standing at his elbow.

Norman nodded, his mouth full of more pie.

"You have your sister to praise for your supper and the pie tonight," Mrs. O'Connor remarked quietly.

"What?" Norman turned from the older woman to Orlena in astonishment. "You made supper and this delicious pie?"

"Only with Mrs. O'Connor's help," Orlena admitted, suddenly feeling a little shy. "It was her idea. I never would have thought of making anything in the kitchen but a mess."

His pie finished, Norman pushed back his chair and put an arm around his sister. "You did a fine job, Sis. I'm proud of you. Keep learning all you can from Mrs. O'Connor and Jenelle." He smiled and then added, "After a meal like I just ate, I don't want to move!" Leaning back in his chair, he watched the ladies clearing off the table. When Orlena returned from the kitchen with a dishcloth to wipe the table, Norman grinned at her.

"See what your cooking has done to me, Sis? It's made me lazy."

Orlena smiled with her lips, but her eyes were sober. She had remembered her attitude of the morning and knew there was something she should do, but she didn't want to.

Standing beside her brother's chair as her dishcloth moved slowly over the table, Orlena suddenly felt his hand on her arm.

"What is it, Orlena?"

Here was her chance. Why was it so hard, she wondered? She drew a deep breath and blurted, "I . . . I'm sorry for arguing with you this morning and complaining." It was out.

Norman turned her gently around and looked her full in the face. "I forgive you, Sis." He pulled her close and hugged her.

A feeling of great relief swept over Orlena, and she relaxed in her brother's embrace. The burden she had carried on her heart all day was gone because she had made things right. She felt free and light.

Pulling away, Orlena shook back her curls and her eyes

sparkled again. "Norman, guess what!"

Sensing her changed mood, Norman smiled. "You caught a fish in the new pond out in what used to be the yard," he guessed.

"No!" Orlena chortled. "Jenelle let me hold Marian today, and she didn't cry!"

"I would hope not." Norman pretended to misunderstand. "Jenelle's a bit too old to cry over sharing her playthings."

The sun was bright and the air warm as Norman Mavrich strode down the main street of Rough Rock. He had ridden into town earlier with his sister and, after leaving the horses at the livery and Orlena at school, had stopped at the general store to purchase a few things Mrs. O'Connor had requested and to pick up the mail. Now as he walked along the muddy street, he kept a sharp look out. There were several men he wanted to meet and one of them, he was sure, would have no desire to meet him. Norman had not forgotten Con Blomberg's unwanted attention towards his sister. However, there was no sign of Blomberg or of his usual companions.

Stopping to chat a few minutes with an acquaintance, Norman saw his friend, Edmund Bruce, leaning against the side of a nearby store, his hat pushed back and his thumbs tucked in his belt, the sole of one booted foot resting against the wall. He gave the appearance of total indifference to what went on around him though he watched every passerby casually.

Nodding in his direction, Norman asked, "By the way, who is that? I don't remember seeing him around here before."

"He's a newcomer in town. Only arrived last week. A drifter some folks say, though he could just be looking for work. Name is Bruce, I think. Um, Edmund Bruce. He's just been hanging around town doing some odd jobs here and there. Seems pretty quiet and doesn't talk much. If you're looking for another hand, Mavrich, you might try him."

"Thanks. I reckon I'll at least talk to him." And touching his hat, Norman moved away.

There was no one else around when Norman stopped before his college friend but, not wanting to risk anything, he said, "Excuse me, my name is Norman Mavrich. Are you new in town?"

"Yep. Name's Bruce."

"Are you looking for work?"

"Maybe," was the non-committal answer.

"I've got a ranch out that direction," and he nodded towards the west. "Spring round-up's likely to be in a week or two, and I could use some more hands. Can you rope?"

"Yep."

"Scared of cattle?"

Bruce snorted. "Nope."

"Ever herded, cut and branded cattle before?"

"Yep."

"Interested in a job?"

"How much?"

Norman named an amount and the other man nodded. "Good. Come out to the Triple Creek later on, and we'll discuss things then. I might have work for you before the round-up, but I might not. I'll let you know." He scribbled something on a piece of paper and held it out. "Directions to the ranch."

Bruce nodded and took the paper, glancing over it casually before slipping it into his pocket.

Without more words, the two men parted with a nod.

"One off my list," Norman muttered to himself. "Now to see the sheriff."

He found him sitting in his office glancing over the morning paper. "Morning, Sheriff."

Sheriff Hughes looked up. "Why, the same to you, Mavrich. What brings you to town this morning? I figured you'd be busy fixing fences and all that other work that comes after such a rain as we had yesterday."

"I would be, but I have a plan, and I wanted to see what you thought of it."

"Well, if it has anything to do with those cattle rustlers, I'm all ears. Hardly anything else has been talked about around here. Pull up a chair and have a seat," he invited cordially.

Accepting the invitation, Norman was soon settled and began. "We've got the Lucky Spur cattle on our ranch now."

"You what?"

"They were brought over yesterday. We saw three men riding off but I don't think they saw us. They had pulled down part of a fence, cut the wires and then later drove the cattle through. One of my men saw them doing the former but he was on foot and alone and there were three of them."

"Good thing he didn't try anything," the sheriff remarked. "What time of day was it and what's your plan?"

Norman told him quickly when and how the fence and extra cattle were discovered and then began to unfold his idea. "Of course, I'll have to talk with Elbert Ledford about it and see if he'll agree to go along."

"It might be a gamble," Sheriff Hughes cautioned. "Are you sure you want to try it?"

CHAPTER 20

A DOUBLE JOB

"There is some risk, of course, of the Bar X losing their cattle, but, so far, all the cattle from the other ranches have ended up on the Triple Creek. It's my cattle that are disappearing, Sheriff. I'm not sure if they are planning to rebrand them or sell them as Triple Creek stock, but if we don't find them, and find them quickly, it's going to cost the Triple Creek a lot of money. I'll admit the plan has its risks, but I haven't thought of a better one."

Slowly Sheriff Hughes nodded his head. "What you say makes sense, Mavrich, and that's the only plan I've heard for catching them that actually might work. I just wish we knew who is behind it all."

Hesitating a moment, Norman glanced out the window and then said, "I think I know at least some of them, Sheriff. That's one reason I think this plan will work. I think it's partly a grudge and a desire for revenge."

The sheriff sat up quickly and looked sharply at his visitor. "What are you talking about, Mavrich?" he demanded. "How did you find out such information?"

"From my secret source." Norman couldn't help smiling. "You know that stranger, Bruce, who has been hanging around town lately?"

"Yep."

"He and I went to college together, and I asked for his

help when he stopped by my place last week. I'd trust him with all I have, Sheriff," Mr. Mavrich added quietly as a doubtful look crossed the sheriff's face. "He got a note to me on Monday."

"What did the note say?"

Pulling a folded bit of paper from his pocket, Norman passed it across the desk to the sheriff who opened it and read:

> Blomberg bragging get even with TC. Seen talking with man called Cass Bishop behind saloon last night. Overheard mention 75 head not bad to start herd. Either man have ranch? Also heard Bishop called "boss" by known gunman.

Silently the sheriff read the note twice and handed it back. "It sure sounds like Blomberg might be involved. Cass Bishop? I wonder what he looks like. And what known gunman was he talking to? I tell you, Mavrich, it's getting harder to keep track of the new folks in town these days!"

"I 'hired' that new fellow for the spring round-up, but told him to stop by the ranch sometime and I might have some work for him. He should be there tonight."

Pushing back his chair, Sheriff Hughes stood up. "Well, you sure move quickly. Mind if I drop by your place this evening?"

"Not at all." Norman had also risen. "Now I've got to ride out to the Bar X and have a chat with Elbert."

Walking his visitor to the door, the sheriff asked, "You think his father will agree to the plans?"

Norman shrugged. "With Ledford down, his sons have taken over the ranch, and Elbert is in charge now. I think the decision will be up to him."

"Well," the sheriff held out his hand, "I'll be seeing you."

The two men shook hands, and Norman started down the street. He had one more stop to make before heading home.

As Norman rode down the lane to the Bar X, he noticed that the place appeared to be more kept up than it had been, but there was no one around when he swung off Captain. After quickly glancing about, he mounted the steps to the kitchen door and knocked. A few minutes later Mrs. Ledford appeared.

"Mr. Mavrich, what brings you all the way out here?" she asked in surprise. "Would you like to come in? I'm afraid Samuel is sleeping now and the boys are off in the north pastures. Could I get you a glass of water?"

Norman smiled, holding his hat in his hand. "No, thank you, ma'am. I came to see Elbert about something, and if you don't mind, I'll just ride out and find him."

"Of course, I don't mind. And congratulations on your new little one. How is Jenelle doing?"

"She's doing quite well, thank you. I know she'd love to have you stop by some day, if you have time."

"Tell her I'll try, but it is hard to get away." And Mrs. Ledford sighed.

Norman smiled. "North pastures, you said?" When she nodded, he added, "Thank you. Good bye." Putting his hat back on as he turned away from the door, Norman swung up into the saddle and, after touching his hat to Mrs. Ledford, rode off for the north part of the ranch.

The sun had dried much of the ground, though it was still soft and large puddles were scattered over low lying areas. The day was bright, and Norman enjoyed the warm sunshine. As he rode, his experienced eye swept over the ranch lands, and he nodded with satisfaction. Elbert Ledford was a quick learner when it came to ranching and he was allowed to do things his own way. "I think he'll make a fine rancher once he gets a few more years under him."

Captain tossed his head in agreement and Norman chuckled. If it hadn't been for the persistent thoughts of rustlers, missing cattle and if his plan would work, Norman would have greatly enjoyed his ride. As it was, however, though he tried to push all troublesome thoughts to the back of his mind, they persisted until, at last, pulling off his hat and slowing Captain, he gazed up into the clear blue sky and spoke aloud.

"Lord, you know the troubles we've got right now with the rustlers. I know I can make plan after plan to catch them, but without your help, they won't work. I'm asking for your help, Father. We don't know how many of them there are, but if You are on our side, it won't matter. Please, Lord, guide these plans, protect the men of the Bar X, Sheriff Hughes and his men, and my men at Triple Creek, and also Bruce. I'm asking this, Father, because you said to cast our cares on you and this has certainly become a care, not just for me, but for many others in the area. Thank you. Amen."

Drawing a long, deep breath, Norman began to whistle as he settled his hat once more on his head and nudged his horse forward.

The sun was beginning to set and still Norman sat around the table in the bunkhouse with his men, Sheriff Hughes and Edmund Bruce. The latter had been introduced to the men as "a new hand for the round-up." "And that's all you are to remember," Mr. Mavrich had instructed seriously.

The men nodded. They knew something was up, and when the sheriff arrived, they were sure of it. St. John had prepared supper for everyone and Norman had eaten with the men, after a talk with the ladies in the house. Now, as they all sat around the table, they listened to Mr. Mavrich outline his plan for catching the rustlers. It wasn't complicated, but it might be dangerous at times if the rustlers turned out to be skilled gunmen too.

"Bruce," Mr. Mavrich turned to his friend, "have you found out anything else since the note?"

The stranger nodded. "Sure have. I've been offered two jobs. Sheriff, should I take 'em both?"

"What are they?"

"One's working for the Triple Creek Ranch. The other

is working for Cass Bishop and Blomberg. I think their business is cattle rustling, and I'd work with Shy Adams."

"Shy Adams!" exclaimed the Sheriff, slapping the table with both hands and sitting up straight. "When did he get in town? How did you learn of him? What's he doing in Rough Rock and who's he working for?"

A murmur had run through the men sitting about the table. "Shy" Shyler Adams was a skilled gunman, often hired for range wars, and well known for his contempt for all lawmen. He had earned his nickname by the silent way he managed to slip in and out of towns, evading any sheriff or deputy. It was also rumored that he spoke more with his guns than his voice. If the rustlers had hired a man like Shy Adams to work for them, they must mean business.

"Bruce, what do you know about this gunman?" Norman asked.

"Not a whole lot, but I've heard of him before and know his reputation. I also know that there's a wanted poster for him in a small town in New Mexico. I overheard a little of the talk between this man and the one who calls himself 'Cass Bishop,' and from what I could gather, Blomberg is paying the money for whatever deal they've got going, Bishop is the brains, and Adams is the head gunman.

"Bishop is the one who talked to me this afternoon. He wanted to know what Mavrich wanted of me. I'm supposed to be double crossing the Triple Creek and feeding information to Bishop, Adams or a few of their other men." Bruce paused and, tipping his head questioningly, added, "I'm not sure Blomberg knows I've been hired on. Perhaps he was too drunk the other day to remember me." He looked around. "That's all I've got to tell."

After his first exclamation of surprise, Sheriff Hughes had listened as intently as the others. When Bruce had finished and leaned back in his chair, the sheriff said slowly, "Mavrich, I'm not sure about this plan any longer if Shy Adams is involved."

Norman nodded slowly. "I know, Sheriff. I reckon we

may have to adjust a few things, but . . ." He paused and slowly tapped his fingers on his knee. "With an inside man, we just may be able to pull it off."

"Where?" Sheriff Hughes wasn't familiar with the land of Triple Creek. "You're going to need a good place to hide, a good place for cattle to be grazing, and a good place that the rustlers don't suspect of being a trap."

"What about Deadlock Canyon?" Hearter suggested.

"It looks too much like a trap," the ranch boss replied.

A few other suggestions were offered, but with each, Norman shook his head with a thoughtful frown.

"Mavrich," Bruce spoke up into the lull which followed the last suggestion by the men, "I think what you need is a wide open valley between two hills and near the border of the ranch. That seems to me the most likely place for them to cut the fence, drive the cattle through and then fix the fence. And, if they drove the cattle through on one side of the ranch before and that's the side you've found the other cattle, I think it's safe to say they'll do it on that side again."

Nodding, Norman agreed. "Yep, we haven't noticed anything on the north side of the ranch. I just wish I knew where they were taking my cattle, because it's pretty certain they are. You did mention in the note about seventy-five head being a good start for a ranch, didn't you?" He reached into his pocket as he spoke and drew out the paper. "Where would they be starting a ranch in this area?"

Norman Mavrich knew the surrounding areas fairly well, as did the sheriff, but neither one could think of an abandoned ranch or even a new one.

"Does this fellow, Blomberg, have a place somewhere?" Bruce asked.

"Sure does," Hardrich answered. "The most rundown piece of land you ever saw. You couldn't feed cattle for more than a month on his land. And if he hasn't fixed the fences, any cattle would be scattered far and wide by sunset."

"Say," Alden put in, "a month would be just about enough time for the cattle to be shipped out by train. Time for the cattle to be rebranded too."

The sheriff promised to look into the matter, being careful not to arouse any suspicions. For another half an hour, the men discussed plans and then Norman said, "Men, I think we need to pray about this. We can't do it on our own, and I don't want any of us starting to think we can. Let's go to our knees and spend some time asking from Him who gives wisdom to those who ask for it."

Edmund Bruce, kneeling beside his school friend, couldn't help contrasting the way this ranch was run with others he had worked on before. With a full heart, he listened as one man after another prayed, not as though it was a duty, but as though they each felt a personal relationship with the One they were talking to. It was no wonder that Norman was willing to listen to their suggestions and let them be a part of the plans; they all relied on the same Fountainhead of Wisdom.

The sheriff departed as soon as they had risen and, after a few more words with his foreman, Mr. Mavrich accompanied his friend to the barn to saddle his horse. "Bruce," he said quietly, as that individual was slipping the bridle on his horse, "I don't like the idea of you working both sides of this problem. Getting information is one thing, but actually working for those men—"

Lifting the saddle, Bruce paused before settling it on his horse's back. "Hey, Mavrich," he chided with a smile in his voice, "someone's got to do it, and it might as well be me."

"Just the same, I don't like it." The horse gave a slight snort. "Neither does Dakota."

Bruce chuckled and patted his horse's neck. Then his voice grew sober as he replied, "I'll admit that I have hesitated a few times about it, but I think it's best if I do it." He finished saddling in silence and then turned to his friend. "Even if something happens to me, Mavrich, I've no one to miss me."

"Don't say that!" Norman's voice was almost harsh.

"Sorry, Norm." Bruce used the name he had used only

on special occasions when the two of them were alone. "I meant I've no wife, children or parents who need me, and if I am to go soon, I'd rather go knowing that I was helping you."

"Ned!" The husky voice couldn't say anything else, and Norman gripped his companion's hand without another word.

The sober mood lasted until the two men reached the barn door, then, as he swung up into the saddle, Bruce remarked, "I'll be here Monday mornin' Boss, but I sure hope I don't have to mend fences 'cause that's such a bother and a waste of time 'cause they're sure ta come down again later."

"Just for that crack, I'll have you fixing fences until you can do it in your sleep," Norman slapped Dakota's side and sent him off down the lane at a gallop.

CHAPTER 21

MISSING HANDS

He stood there in the darkness watching until the shadowy form disappeared. Turning back to the barn, Norman made sure things were settled for the night before shutting the barn door and starting towards the house.

It was later than he thought, for as he entered the kitchen, Norman heard the clock strike the hour. Hanging up his hat, he took the lit lamp Mrs. O'Connor had left on the table and quietly made his way through the dark and sleeping house up to his room. As he thought, Jenelle was awake and waiting for him.

"Sorry I was gone so long, Sweet," Norman whispered, bending down to kiss her. "We had a lot to talk over then we spent some time in prayer."

Jenelle smiled tenderly. "Do you feel better now?" she asked, reaching up and resting her hand against her husband's face.

Turning his head, Norman kissed the small hand before imprisoning it in his own. "Yes," he replied. "I'm still worried about Edmund though," he admitted. "I almost wish I hadn't asked him to help."

"Are you second guessing yourself, Dear?"

"That's exactly what I am doing, and I shouldn't, I know. I'll leave it all with the Lord and get some sleep. There are busy days ahead of us," Norman yawned. "Very busy."

Friday was a beautiful day. By afternoon the sun, shining from a sky streaked with thin, white clouds, felt almost hot after only an hour of work. Norman was repairing one of the corrals near the barn with Greg and Burns, who had almost fully recovered from his exposure in Tuesday's storm, when Hardrich strode towards them and called out, "Mavrich, have you seen Davis around?"

Straightening, Norman pulled out his bandana and mopped his face. "No, not since he rode out this morning. Why?"

Reaching the three men, the ranch foreman rested an elbow on a post and asked, "He was only out on patrol, wasn't he?"

Norman nodded and glanced up at the sun. "Lloyd, Alden and Maynard rode out to take over patrols over an hour ago. The others should be back."

"That's what has me wondering. Tracy and Barker have returned, but neither one had seen any sign of Davis, and he hasn't returned."

For a moment, Norman stood in thought. Then he spoke. "Tell Scott to saddle up his horse and the two of us will ride out and see what's become of him. Perhaps Shadow went lame. It'd be a long way to walk." He turned to Burns and Greg. "You two keep working here. I'll send St. John out to help if he's not still busy in the barn."

By the time Norman, having stopped at the pump to fill his canteen, arrived at the barn, Scott had Captain and Star saddled and ready to go. As the two men mounted and rode off, Scott asked, "Where was Davis patrolling?"

"Out past Penny Creek. Lloyd's out there now, and there might not be anything wrong, but—well, Davis is getting older, and he's not as strong as he'd have us believe."

"You think something happened to him?" Scott asked.

"I don't know. Shad could have gone lame, or thrown a shoe, or . . ." The sentence trailed off as though Norman couldn't quite put his thoughts into words.

"Or Davis could have run into the rustlers."

"Yep."

For a quarter of an hour the two men rode, not pushing their mounts, but moving at a steady pace, pausing at the top of each rise to scan the ranch lands for any sign of the older cowhand. When each hilltop brought another disappointment, Norman began to feel uneasy. Crossing Penny Creek, the men were silent, until Norman suddenly pointed ahead.

"Over there, Scott. Isn't that Davis's horse?"

Scott was already urging Star forward until he neared the horse who was grazing all alone. "Shad," Scott called quietly.

The horse raised his head, his ears turning towards the approaching riders.

"Come on, boy," Scott coaxed, holding out his hand.

Quite willingly, Shadow ambled over and allowed Scott to catch his reins.

Norman pulled up on the other side of the horse. "Check him over, Scott, I'll hold him."

After passing the reins over to the ranch boss, Scott dismounted and began running his hands over the horse's legs checking for injuries and lifting his feet to see if he'd lost a shoe. Finding nothing wrong, he straightened. "There's nothing the matter with him, sir."

"Except that his rider seems to be missing," Norman replied grimly, scanning the fields in all directions.

Scott didn't answer.

"We haven't seen any sign of Hearter either. Scott, let's try following Shad's trail and see if it'll lead us to Davis."

The trail wasn't too hard to follow, but it wandered here and there for a while and there was still no sign of Mack Davis. The men were nearing Deadlock Canyon when the trail disappeared, which wasn't surprising since the ground around there was rocky. Drawing rein, Mr. Mavrich sat alertly in his saddle, his keen grey eyes studying something in the canyon. Instinctively his hand slid to the holstered gun at his side.

"Do you see something, sir?" Scott asked in a low voice.

Without taking his eyes off the canyon, Norman dismounted. "I'm not sure. Take my horse and wait here."

"Mr. Mavrich, I—" Scott took the reins reluctantly. He had slipped from his horse when Norman had and now drew his own six-shooter. He didn't like the idea of Mr. Mavrich entering the canyon alone, but there was really nothing he could do except follow orders and wait and pray.

Cautiously, Norman, his drawn gun in his hand, made his way into the canyon, taking care to stay in the shadow of the rocks and few scrub bushes. He could see what appeared to be a horse standing in the shade of an overhanging rock, but from where he was, he couldn't be sure if he recognized it or not. Creeping slowly forward, trying to avoid loose rocks which might slide, Norman didn't forget to look on the ridges higher up to see if anyone was watching his progress. But he could see no one. The closer he drew to the horse, the more certain he became that it was Spitfire.

"Then where's Lloyd?" Norman asked himself. "He's got to be around somewhere." He didn't dare call out lest the young hand was being held prisoner by the rustlers. Pausing, he wondered if he could get close enough to the overhang to see in without being seen and without Spitfire giving his presence away. After a quick, silent prayer for protection, Norman Mavrich started forward, farther into Deadlock Canyon. The slightest noise of a pebble shifting as he stepped on it, the rustling of the wind in the bushes, even the buzzing of a fly, was, to his taut nerves, as loud as a shout. A dozen yards away from the horse, Spitfire lifted his head and gave a soft, friendly nicker of welcome.

"Come out of there with your hands up!" Norman's

sharp voice rang like a pistol shot into the silence of the canyon and the echos bounced from rocky ledge to canyon walls.

"Mr. Mavrich?"

"Lloyd!" Norman exclaimed as the young man stepped around his horse. "What's the matter? What happened?" he demanded at sight of the anxious face before him.

Hearter beckoned him in. "It's Davis. He's been shot, and it's real bad."

Taking a step forward, Norman suddenly turned, cupped his hands around his mouth and bellowed, "Scott!"

In the shadow of the overhang, Norman's quick eyes saw the older man, lying on the rocky ground, his face white and his eyes closed. He also noticed another man, a stranger, sitting on the ground, his hands behind him, but the ranch boss scarcely gave him more than a passing glance; his entire attention was on the injured man.

Quickly he knelt down beside him and opened the blood soaked shirt.

"I tried to staunch the blood, but I think I've only checked it," Lloyd whispered. "I'm glad you got here when you did, sir."

Norman didn't reply, he was examining the wound. It was bad and, though not as bad as he had first feared, Davis was going to need a doctor and as quickly as possible.

The injured man stirred slightly, moaned and opened his eyes. "Mavrich?"

"Yes, Davis, I'm here," Norman said quietly.

"I found the rustler's way . . . just one of 'em . . . Shadow . . ."

"Easy, Davis," Norman soothed. "We found Shadow. He's just fine."

"Water."

Scott had ridden up with the other horses, and a canteen was quickly held to the older man's lips. He drank some and then his eyes closed once more and his hand, which had grasped Norman's, went limp.

Anxiously, Norman felt for his pulse. It was weak but steady, and he breathed a sigh of relief. Turning to Scott and Hearter, he again noticed the stranger who had not said a word the whole time. "Who is he?"

Hearter shrugged. "I don't know. He was tied up near Davis when I found them. And he won't talk."

"We'll find out later." Mr. Mavrich's words became quick and decisive. "Hearter, ride for the doctor. Change horses at the barn if you need to. Don't tell anyone in town anything except that there was an accident and Doc French is needed."

"Yes, sir!" Vaulting into the saddle, Lloyd set Spitfire in motion with a touch of his heels.

"Scott, find some poles we can tie together to make a litter. We've got to get Davis back to the house. And Scott," he added as the ranch hand turned to go, "keep your gun ready and your eyes and ears open."

Scott nodded and disappeared.

Left alone with a seriously injured man and a silent stranger who was tied up, Norman shook his head. He wished he had brought along St. John as well as Scott, but that couldn't be changed now. After checking Davis's pulse once more and seeing that the flow of blood seemed staunched for the time, he rose and moved over to the silent man.

He checked the ropes which bound his hands. They were tied well. He noticed a stained handkerchief tied clumsily around one leg.

"You hurt?" he asked.

There was no answer.

Shrugging, Norman quickly undid the makeshift bandage and raised his eyebrows. Another gunshot wound met his eyes, and he glanced quickly at the stranger. The man wasn't even looking at him, but was staring down at his belt. Norman saw the empty holster and made a few mental guesses about what had happened.

"What's your name?" he asked.

Again there was no reply from the stranger.

Reaching for the canteen, Norman offered him a drink, but the man gave no response except to turn his head slightly away. With a shrug, Norman pulled off his bandana, and using some of the water from the canteen, began to wash the blood away from the wound. The man winced and then clenched his jaw.

'You still have a bullet in there," Norman remarked quietly though he didn't expect any answer. "We'll get you back to the ranch and have Doc take care of it."

"Get it out."

Norman Mavrich looked up. They were the first words the stranger had spoken. For a moment he just looked at him, trying to read what was passing through the stranger's mind, but his face was half turned away and hard to see in the shadows.

Just then a shout sounded down the canyon. "Mr. Mavrich!"

Springing up quickly, Norman hurried into the sun and squinted into its brightness. "Maynard!" he exclaimed, as the young man leapt from his horse and pushed past Captain and Star to reach his boss. "What are you doing here?"

Breathing heavily, Maynard gasped out, "I met Hearter riding for the ranch. All I caught was something about you and the canyon and going for Doc." He heaved a sigh of relief. "I thought something had happened to you, sir."

"Not to me, but Davis is pretty bad. Scott is looking for something to use for a stretcher to carry him back. And we have someone else who's been shot in the leg. Bullet's still in there."

By this time, the two men had re-entered the shade of the overhanging rock. Davis moaned and his boss knelt down beside him.

"Mavrich . . ."

"I'm here, Davis. Don't try to talk now. Save your strength for the trip home."

The injured man didn't seem to hear. "Thought I'd pay

back . . . money I . . . stole. Found rustler's . . . secret. But where . . ." He turned his head slowly, and his breathing became labored.

"Hush, Davis," Norman soothed, "we'll talk later. You just rest now."

For a moment the man's eyes rested on the concerned face above him. He smiled faintly and murmured, "If I don't make it . . . tell the missus good-bye."

"Davis! You can't go. I need you. Don't give up now. Hang on, Davis, hang on a little longer!" The pleading in Mr. Mavrich's voice was full of half suppressed emotion, and he whispered, "Please, Lord, not yet. Don't take him yet!"

When Scott arrived with two slender but sturdy poles, Norman didn't have time to give directions, for Maynard already had a rope and a blanket from off his horse. Quickly the men worked in swift silence and then, with gentle hands, they lifted their fallen comrade onto the litter and covered him with the blanket.

It was only after Davis was ready that Norman turned his attention to the stranger. Pulling out his handkerchief, he rapidly but skillfully splinted and bound up the leg again. "Doc can take care of it later," he told him.

The man didn't answer.

"Maynard," Mr. Mavrich directed, "help him onto one of the horses. Then you mount up and take him to the bunkhouse. Take the other horses along, and Scott and I will follow on foot with Davis. You'll get there before we will, so send a few other men out with the light wagon for us."

"Yes, sir."

Norman held a gun on the stranger as Maynard and Scott helped him up on Star and then tied his hands to the pommel. Holding the reins for all the horses, Maynard sprang on his horse and nudged him forward, keeping beside the stranger. "Don't try anything," he warned as they rode off towards the entrance to the canyon.

Stooping to check the pulse of Davis once more, Norman said quietly, "Scott, I still can't figure out how the stranger could be tied up and Davis so badly injured."

"Hearter didn't tie the man up?"

"He says not. But let's get going. We've got a long walk ahead."

T

It wasn't until the middle of the following morning that Dr. French declared Mack Davis out of danger. "It was close, and I wasn't too sure he'd pull through," he admitted soberly. "He's still going to need a lot of careful nursing before he's on his feet again. I hear young Hearter was the first one to his aid?" As Norman nodded, he continued. "If he hadn't gotten there when he did, I don't think I could have done anything."

"When can I talk with him, Doc?" Norman's face was serious.

"As soon as he wakes up, if you like, but on no account is he to get out of that bed!"

"I'll see to it that he follows those orders, sir. And how is Ky?" The stranger had said his name was Ky, but what he was doing on the Triple Creek Ranch, he wouldn't say, nor would he tell what had happened between himself and Mack Davis. Norman had his own ideas, but wisely kept them to himself and his foreman.

"Oh, Ky'll be fine given some more rest. Where did you say he came from?"

"I didn't say. Do you recognize him, Doc?"

Frowning, Dr. French shook his head slowly. "Nope, I can't say that I do. Should I?"

"Not necessarily," Norman replied.

"You want me to notify the sheriff for you?" Dr. French looked questioningly at the younger man.

The master of Triple Creek Ranch shook his head. "No. The men will see to it that he doesn't leave his bed, and I don't want word of this mentioned to anyone. The sheriff deputized Hardrich and myself for the time being."

The doctor nodded and said he wanted to check on Mrs. Mavrich and the baby since he was at the ranch and, after a few words with Hardrich, Norman led the way inside.

Jenelle was greatly relieved to hear the report on Mack Davis. "I wish he were at the house so I could help nurse him," she sighed.

"That's one reason I took him directly to the bunkhouse." Her husband smiled while the doctor grunted.

CHAPTER 22

UNABLE TO LOVE

The day was drawing slowly to a close, the evening meal was finished, and Mrs. O'Connor and Orlena were washing the dishes as Norman left the ranch house and headed across the yard. Lloyd had just brought word that Mack Davis was awake and wanted to talk. A few of the men were sitting outside when Norman arrived at the bunkhouse, but they quickly followed him inside. All were eager to hear what Davis had to say, for Ky hadn't said a word, but lay in the bed where he had been placed, silent and withdrawn.

Crossing the room, Norman glanced at the two injured men and wondered how close his guesses had been about what had happened. "Good evening, Davis," he greeted his older hand quietly. "How are you feeling?"

"I'm afraid I ain't gonna be able to ride a horse tomorrow, boss. It sure is mighty strange. I could ride jest fine last night, but this night I'm stuck in bed."

Mr. Mavrich exchanged glances with Hardrich before replying, "Last night, Davis, you were in this bed, unconscious."

"Well, I—what's that, sir?" And the sick man looked startled. "You mean I've been in this here bed since yesterday?"

Smiling, Norman nodded.

Turning his head, Davis looked at the other men

gathered about the room. It took a few minutes for this news to sink in but when it did, Davis gave a start and then groaned at the sudden movement.

"Easy, Davis," Norman cautioned, placing a hand on his shoulder. "Just relax and don't do anything more than talk."

For a minute Davis lay with his eyes closed. "Mavrich," he said at last, opening his eyes, "who found me?"

"Hearter did."

"Was anyone else about?"

"Yes, Ky was there with his hands tied behind him and a bullet in his leg."

"Where's that cattle thief now?" Davis demanded.

"Suppose you just tell us what happened," Norman suggested. He sat down on a stool next to the bed. "We'll talk about the other man later."

"I remembered another time years ago," Davis began. "This were back when yer uncle was runnin' the ranch. And there were some rustlers then. I jest recalled how they done operated. Figured it might be the same way this time."

Jim Hardrich joined the ranch boss by the injured man's bed. "You mean that time when they'd take a few head at a time, drive them through Deadlock Canyon and out that narrow gully?"

"Yep." Davis nodded, frowning as even that slight movement sent sharp stabs of pain through his body. "I decided to see if I were right, an' I caught that fella startin' to drive four or five head through the canyon. I didn't see anyone else, so thought I could stop him. We both fired at the same time. I knew I was hit, but I done see him fall and managed ta get to him. He weren't kilt like I first thought, jest knocked hisself out hittin' his head, so I took his gun an' tied his hands. I saw he were bleedin' pretty bad, an' I wanted ta stop it, but I were so dizzy I ain't sure I ever did. An' I don't recall a thing more till I woke up in this bed with the doc and Mavrich beside me. Now what happened to the cattle thief? And how'd I get here?"

Quietly Norman filled him in on how he had been found and rescued along with the cattle thief and then he added, his face grave. "What you did, Davis, was brave but foolish. You might have been killed. If you hadn't been found when you were, we wouldn't be here talking now. Trying to capture a rustler on your own. Humph!" He looked sternly around to include the rest of the men. "From now on, until this group is caught, I don't want anyone going off alone. You'll at least stay in earshot of each other. Is that clear?" Heads nodded. "Good. Because if any one of you tries to pull a stunt like Davis did, you'll get the worst tongue lashing you ever had and it might cost you your place at the Triple Creek."

Into the silence which followed Mr. Mavrich's words, came the low voice of Davis. "Mavrich, I wasn't doin' it jest because. I got a debt I owe the Triple Creek an' I were thinkin' of that."

Norman's face lost its stern look, and he placed a hand lightly over the hand of the older man. "Davis, that debt is canceled. Your life is worth more to me and to my wife than any amount of money." He rose. "Now get some rest."

Davis gave a tired smile, and his eyes closed.

Turning from that bed, Mr. Mavrich stepped across to another where the injured stranger lay. "How's the leg tonight?" he asked quietly.

Turning his head, the man looked up silently and said not a word.

"If you need anything or want to talk, just let one of my men know." Briefly, Norman placed a kind hand on the man's shoulder. When the man still remained silent, Norman turned away, said a few words to his men and then, followed by his foreman, left the bunkhouse.

"Do you want anyone on patrol tonight?" Hardrich asked.

Norman glanced at the western sky where the sun was going down, a shimmering ball of gold sinking in a rose and orange colored sky. He nodded. "I reckon we ought to have someone out around here. These rustlers may be after the cattle, but I'd hate to lose some of the horses too. And remember, the men are to go out in twos. I can't stand the loss of another good hand."

"I'll see to it," promised Hardrich. "Any other instructions?"

The men talked for a few minutes more, and then Norman crossed the yard and returned to the house.

₡

Orlena was waiting in the church yard for Mrs. O'Connor to finish talking with Mrs. Kirby after Sunday services. Norman had remained back at the ranch with Jenelle, and had sent Mr. Hardrich and Lloyd Hearter with them. Lloyd had gone to visit his mother with Charity and Connie as soon as church was over, and Orlena was alone. As she stood watching some boys chasing each other around a few trees, someone came up beside her.

"You and your brother are just alike!" the voice hissed.

Orlena whirled around in surprise. Elvira stood before her with flashing eyes and her hands on her hips. Completely bewildered by this sudden attack, Orlena could only gasp, "What are you talking about?"

"You know very well what I'm talking about, Orlena Mavrich!" snapped the furious girl. "You tried to be nice to me so I'd let you borrow my books, and then you made up a lie about them so you could keep them and get me in trouble. Now," she hurried on before Orlena could speak, "your brother has been pretending to help Elbert run our ranch, and all the time he was planning last night's events."

"What happened last night?"

Elvira snorted. "Don't play innocent. Your brother arranged to have fifteen head of Bar X cattle stolen, that's what."

"Why do you think it was my brother?" demanded Orlena, beginning to grow angry. "It could have been, and probably was, the rustlers, and you know it!"

"Huh, no one believes there really are rustlers," Elvira taunted. "Just how many head of cattle has the Triple Creek lost?"

"I don't know."

"See, of course it's your brother. Oh, I'm not saying he does it himself, but he does all the planning, I'm sure. Why, our missing cattle are probably on the Triple Creek now just waiting to be rebranded. How else could—"

"Elvira!" Edgar came up behind her. "Mother is ready to go."

"All right. I'll be right there."

Elvira's smile was fake, and Orlena knew it. She wondered if Edgar realized that something was going on, for he frowned slightly as he turned away, and Orlena saw him glance once or twice over his shoulder.

"Pa doesn't know about the missing cattle yet," Elvira hissed, "but if he has another attack when he finds out, it'll be all your brother's fault! And if Pa dies, your brother will have killed him!" With this final insult, Elvira turned on her heel and hurried to the carriage where her mother and brother were waiting.

Left alone, Orlena stared after them, trying to take in what she had just heard. It couldn't be true. She felt her face flush and bit her lips to keep from shouting after the retreating carriage. How dare Elvira make such accusations against her brother! "Just wait until school tomorrow, I'll teach you—" Orlena's muttering stopped short as a verse in the morning's sermon echoed in her head.

"Love covereth a multitude of sins."

Did she really love Elvira? Right then Orlena knew she didn't, and she wasn't even sure she wanted to try any longer to be kind to her.

When Mrs. O'Connor called her, she was still fuming inwardly. One minute she was mentally calling Elvira a liar and thinking of what she could do to her, and the next she was trying to forget all about what she had heard.

So busy were her thoughts that she spoke not a word on the drive home, and even during dinner she was silent. In spite of the trust she had in her brother, Elvira's words had planted tiny seeds of doubt in her mind, and the more she fumed inside and tried to argue the accusations away by herself, the more the doubts grew.

Restlessly, after the dishes were washed, Orlena wandered the house and, at last, finding herself out on the porch, dropped down on a step and leaned her elbows on her knees.

Inside, Norman was speaking to Mrs. O'Connor. "Did something happen at church or in town? Orlena hasn't said a word since you returned."

"Sure and I've been wondering myself what's going on entirely. The child hasn't spoken in my hearing since church was dismissed."

A minute later the kitchen door opened, and Orlena heard a step on the porch behind her. She didn't turn her head, but out of the corner of her eye she saw a pair of boots slowly come down the steps and then stop. Norman sat down beside her.

"That sun feels pleasant," he remarked.

Orlena didn't answer.

"How was church this morning?"

Again there was no answer. Orlena didn't dare trust herself to speak because her temper was trying to get the better of her and some of the hands were enjoying the sunshine too.

"Orlena, what's wrong?" Norman placed a hand on her arm as he spoke.

Springing abruptly to her feet, she snapped tensely, "The same thing it's been!" and then stormed off across the yard.

Drawing a deep breath, Norman watched her go and then rising, he followed. Past the barn and the corrals, up the small hill and then down into the group of trees near the stream. This was the first place Orlena had enjoyed at the ranch and, even though it was also where she had encountered the skunk, she often returned to the shady place, even more so now that spring had brought warmer weather.

Flinging herself down on a rock near the water, Orlena tried to calm herself. Why hadn't she asked Elvira what her brothers had said? What if they thought the same thing about Norman?

"All right, Orlena, what is going on?" Norman's quiet voice startled her, and she realized that he had seated himself beside her on the rock.

"It's Elvira."

Norman looked over at her. "Yes?" When no answer came, he said quietly, "Just tell me everything that happened and get it off your mind. It's not going to help you to let it fester."

Clenching her hands, Orlena blurted, "She said you were the one stealing all the cattle and if her father dies it would be you who killed him, and I wanted to slap her, but I didn't, and I don't want to be kind to her ever again!" Crossing her arms, Orlena glared down at the water. "I can't be nice to her after what she said, so don't ask me to. And she said the Bar X cattle were probably on the Triple Creek right now and that I'd just made up a lie about those dime novels so I could keep them and get her in trouble!" Orlena was upset, and now that she had begun to talk, the words just poured out while her brother sat in silence listening. "She said that the only reason you were pretending to help at the Bar X was so that you could steal their cattle and everyone thinks that you are behind all the stealing that's going on! And I didn't do anything to stop her! But you aren't stealing the cattle, are you? Or planning things so others do it for you?" She turned a distressed face up to her brother.

"No, Orlena," Norman reassured quietly. "I'm working to catch the cattle thieves, not help them."

"I wish I didn't have to speak to Elvira again!"

"Do you?"

Orlena looked confused, "Do I what?"

"Have to speak to her again?"

"I . . . I . . . What do you mean?"

Norman wasn't interested in just giving his sister pat answers to her problems, he wanted her to be able to think things out for herself. "Do you have to speak to her in school?"

"No, I guess not."

"Couldn't you just ignore her there and everywhere else?"

"Yes, but—" She paused and leaned her cheek on her hand as she stared at the cool, clear water of the stream as it danced in its bed, sparkling in the sunlight. "That wouldn't be right, would it?"

"Would it?" Norman's grey eyes were fastened on his sister's face.

Slowly a full five minutes passed and Orlena didn't say a word, but her troubled face showed that her mind was busy. Norman waited quietly, praying silently for wisdom to help his sister.

"Oh, I don't know!" Orlena wailed at last. "I don't want to love her or be kind to her, but Reverend Kirby said this morning that love covers sins and the Bible says to love people. But I don't think I can! And are people really thinking that you are one of the rustlers? What if someone does find cattle in the pasture that don't belong to the Triple Creek? Oh, I don't know what to think!" The poor, bewildered girl burst into tears.

Putting an arm about his sister, Norman let her cry on his shirt for a few minutes. When she was calmer, he said, "No, Orlena, you can't love Elvira. You can't even like her. But Christ can. And if you are willing to let Him love her through you, He will. But you have to be willing." He let his words sink in before adding, "Do you want to be willing?"

Wordlessly she nodded, her face hidden from sight.

"One more question. Are you willing to forgive

Elvira?"

Orlena's head came up and her face, streaked with tears, was astonished. "Forgive her?" she gasped. "But she's said such nasty things about you and has been so mean." A tear trickled down her cheek.

Handing her his handkerchief, Norman said quietly, "Christ forgave you because He loved you. Were you any better than Elvira Ledford?"

"But I can't," was the whimpered reply.

"Do you want to?"

Lifting troubled eyes to her brother's face, Orlena whispered, "Yes, but I can't."

CHAPTER 23

TRAILING THIEVES

"If Christ can love Elvira through you, He can help you forgive her. Do you want to kneel down here and ask Him?"

The sheltered, shady spot next to the stream was turned into a sacred place and the rock became an altar that day as Orlena knelt there beside her brother, asking for help to forgive Elvira. "Lord Jesus," she prayed, "I can't love Elvira. I've tried and tried and I can't. But Norman said that You can love her through me. Please do it because right now I can't love her, and I don't want to, but I know I should. So, please, love her as You loved me."

Norman prayed after Orlena had finished and then they both rose. Orlena heaved a long sigh and leaned against her brother.

"Do you feel better now?" he asked. When she nodded, he added, "Orlena, I think you have some rustlers in your own life."

Orlena looked up in astonishment. "What do you mean?"

"A rustler is someone who steals. In most cases he's stealing cattle or horses, but I think there is another kind too, only this kind steals your joy and your peace. When you neglect your Bible or your prayers, you are letting down your guard so the rustlers can come in and steal from you. When you allow unkind thoughts to dwell in your mind, they begin to rob you. Anything that comes into your life and begins to take away your contentment, your joy, your peace, or even your love for someone else, should not be allowed to remain. You know the trouble the cattle rustlers are causing the ranches around here and how we're working to stop them."

She nodded.

"Well, the next time you notice your joy or peace missing, go to the Lord for help to track down and catch the rustlers in your life. All right?"

"Yes, I will. But, Norman, do others really think you're one of the rustlers?"

Norman gave a slight laugh and admitted frankly, "I don't know. But don't worry about what others are saying right now. Several of us are working to catch the rustlers. Including Elbert Ledford, only his sister probably doesn't know it."

Wiping her eyes, Orlena sniffed. "Then why did Elvira say the Bar X lost fifteen head last night?"

"I wouldn't worry about it, if I were you." He hugged her. "Just forget all talk of rustlers and stolen cattle, all right?" When she nodded, Norman added, "Why don't we head back to the house? If Jenelle's awake, we can pay her and Marian a visit."

To this suggestion Orlena agreed. Walking back, her hand held in her brother's, she asked, "Did you ever get tired of school and wish it would end?"

Norman laughed heartily. "I most certainly did! But somehow I managed to live through the last days each year."

The visit with Jenelle and Baby Marian was enjoyable and that night, after Orlena was ready for bed, she sat in her chair beside the window and gazed up at the stars. Something Rev. Kirby had said in his sermon came to mind: "God knows each star by name." Leaning on the windowsill, she mused, "If God cares enough about the stars to name each one, then He must have enough love for Elvira."

The house was dark. The entire ranch seemed to be sleeping that Tuesday night, and even the moon was just a sliver in the sky as someone quietly pushed opened the kitchen door of the ranch house and slipped inside.

"Mavrich?" a voice whispered.

"Right here," came the equally quiet reply, and from the dark corner Norman stepped forward. "You think they bought it?"

"Pretty sure of it. But to be cautious, I went directly back to the bunkhouse and waited."

"Good. I wish we had had more time to get this plan in place, but something had to be done. Spring round-ups are already starting on some of the ranches and I dared not wait any longer."

"How are you going to get word to the Sheriff?"

"I'm not. Too risky. But he knows what we planned. Now we'd better get some sleep before tomorrow."

The two men said a low good night and one slipped from the dark kitchen out into the equally dark night. Norman Mavrich stood by the window and watched. The man slipped from shadow to shadow, pausing now and then to listen before moving on.

Before going upstairs to bed, Norman knelt there in the kitchen. "Lord, our plans have been made, and it's up to You if they are to succeed. Please help us, Father. Amen."

"How much longer do you think we'll have to wait, Hardrich?" Hearter asked. "Spitfire doesn't like this inaction." The men were gathered behind a hill with their mounts, ready to follow any rustlers who might show up.

"Neither do you," Triple Creek's foreman retorted with a slight smile. Then his face grew serious again. "I don't know how long it will be. It could be another hour."

"We've already been here at least an hour," muttered Barker. "I'm ready for something to happen."

"Aren't we all," Greg agreed.

There was a snort from one of the horses and Hardrich turned in the saddle. "Scott, can't you keep Minuet quiet?"

The wrangler shook his head. "I'm trying, sir, but she's not interested in me. Here, Lloyd, you try." And he passed the reins over. Norman's usual horse, Captain, had thrown a shoe the day before and bruised his foot, forcing Norman to choose a different mount. He had chosen Minuet.

"It's time she spent the day under a saddle," he had said. "Besides, I may want her speed."

Under Lloyd's quiet talk, the chestnut mustang soon settled down. The men continued to wait, most of them resting on the hillside while their horses grazed.

The long stretch of fence line, which the new hand, Edmund Bruce, was patrolling, stretched out in the valley below. From their hidden vantage point on top of the hill, Norman, St. John and Tompkins waited and watched. Norman had been there since before Bruce had begun his patrol and the others had come up only ten minutes before to relieve Alden and Maynard.

"Mavrich," Tompkins whispered, "what if they suspect a trap and go to another part of the ranch?"

"Then we'll keep trying. But I don't think they will. The only reason they might have for suspicion is if they went looking for Ky or someone starts to doubt Bruce. I have a feeling though that something is going to happen, and happen soon."

Bruce rode into view and a gentle breeze carried the sound of his singing up to the hidden men. It was a song he must have learned when he was in New Mexico, for the chorus seemed to be in Spanish. The singing stopped abruptly, and Bruce was seen pulling up his horse. The men on the hillside froze. Was he about to give the signal that he had seen something? There it was; he took off his hat, wiped his face with his handkerchief, replaced his hat and began to whistle as he rode off.

"They're coming!" St. John breathed.

"Keep your eyes open," Norman ordered softly.

In silence the three men froze in their hideout, scarcely even daring to breathe lest it betray them to the approaching riders. Below them, Bruce was riding away from the fence and was soon out of sight, leaving the area free for the rustlers. Apparently not one of the three riders suspected anything, for they rode boldly up to the fence, cut the wires, and began driving the cattle through the gap. There were fifteen head, as Norman had guessed there would be. He couldn't tell from that distance but he was certain that the brands would all be those of the Bar X. The riders wore their hats low and had tied bandanas around their faces, so it was impossible to tell for certain who the men were.

In tones scarcely audible, Mr. Mavrich remarked, "That nearest horse looks a bit like Gross's. Wish I could see his face. Don't recognize the other horses though. Do you?"

St. John and Tompkins responded in the negative, their eyes remaining on the action below them.

After what seemed like hours to the watching men, the fence was restrung and the three riders turned and rode quickly away.

Still keeping low, Norman Mavrich moved along the ridge, watching the disappearing figures. At last, he turned. "All right, let's get to the horses."

St. John and Tompkins needed no other words but quickly scrambled down the rather steep slope to where the others were waiting with growing impatience.

"Where's Bruce?" Norman asked Hardrich as he reached for Minuet's reins.

"I haven't seen him."

Anxiously Norman scanned the men gathered around, searching for the face of his friend, but he didn't see it. "He knew where to meet us," he muttered with a frown. Should they wait a few more minutes or trust that Bruce would follow and catch up with them? For a moment Norman hesitated. Then he made his decision. "Let's ride!"

At a light touch of the spurs, Minuet leaped forward and led the way down the gully, around the hill, and out onto the open range beyond, the other horses eagerly following. When the cattle came into view, Mr. Mavrich ordered his men to halt. "Hardrich, Alden and Greg, go check the brands on those cattle. St. John, Tracy, Hearter and Wilson, cut the fence over there near those bushes so we can ride out, and be ready to restring it once we're out. Maynard, as soon as the fence is cut, go out and start tracking. Barker, Burns, ride with him and keep your eyes open for any trouble. Scott, Tompkins, wait with me."

Rapidly the men rushed to obey their orders, leaving Mr. Mavrich and his two men waiting and watching. Norman hoped Bruce would catch up with them, and his gaze moved swiftly in every direction, searching for a dun colored horse and its rider.

As Hardrich, Alden and Greg rode back to their waiting boss a short time later, Hardrich called out, "They're all Bar X like we figured they'd be."

"Good." Norman gave a quick nod and turned once more to scan the far ranch lands in hopes of seeing Bruce. A shout from the men at the fence was heard. "Well, we can't wait any longer. Let's go."

Quickly the men turned towards the gap in the fence. All were eager to follow the unknown riders and put a stop once and for all to the cattle rustling.

Keeping his mount beside Minuet, Hardrich asked quietly, "You worried about Bruce?"

"A little. Wish I knew where he was." And Norman glanced behind them. "I don't like the idea of him riding after us alone. But," he gave a slight pull to his hat, "we've got to ride while the trail's still hot."

The men had been riding for what felt like hours at a steady pace, following the trail of the three riders. Suddenly Maynard, who was riding in the lead, reined up and dismounted.

"What's up?" Norman demanded.

"They've left the trail they came in on. See," the ranch hand pointed straight ahead, "they came from that way with the cattle, but here they've turned off."

"Hmm, I wonder why they did that. Whoa, Minuet," Norman backed his horse a few steps, for the chestnut was prancing and trying to take the bit in her mouth. "Easy girl. We haven't decided which way to go yet."

"You think they know we're following them, Mavrich?" Hardrich asked.

"Could be. Or it could be just a precaution, or . . ." his sentence trailed off as he scanned the surrounding landscape.

"Or what, sir?" Lloyd asked.

Without looking at him, Norman replied, "If you had taken cattle from a pasture and were returning without them, would you ride back to the pasture or head to the barn?"

"So, you think we're near the hideout?" Scott asked, catching on to what his boss had in mind.

"Well, we might be. It's hard saying. Hardrich, I think we ought to—" What Norman thought was interrupted by Burns.

"Mavrich! There's a lone rider approaching from behind!"

Minuet danced in a half circle at the pressure of her rider's legs. Squinting against the sun's glare, Norman rested his hand on his holstered gun. The rider was too far distant to tell if he was friend or foe; however, as he drew nearer, Norman relaxed. "I'd say that was Bruce."

"That's what I was thinking, sir," Scott said quietly. "I recognize the horse."

When Bruce pulled up his buckskin gelding, he took off his hat, wiped his face and said, "Dakota and I were beginning to think we'd never catch up with you."

"What held you up? Did you notice anything about the three riders that might identify them? Did you recognize them?"

Bruce shook his head at Norman's questions and took a drink. "I'll tell you what happened later. What's up now?" Quickly the situation was explained. "I think we should divide up and follow both trails," he suggested.

"My thoughts exactly. Hardrich, you take Greg, Barker, Tracy, Burns, Scott and Wilson and follow the trail the cattle took. The rest of you follow me. And all of you, keep your guns ready and ride quiet. Let's go."

Keeping a sharp lookout, the men followed their ranch boss along the trail made by the three riders.

"They don't appear to have been in a hurry," was Maynard's low comment after some time had passed with still no sign of buildings, camp or even a fence.

Reaching the top of a low rise, Norman held up his hand and the men pulled their horses to a stop. "I think we may see some action soon. If I'm not mistaken, just beyond that farther rise and behind those trees, is Blomberg's place. I had a feeling this was where we were headed." He drew his rifle. "Get your guns out men. If Shy Adams is around, there are bound to be fireworks."

"Where do you think the other trail led, sir?" Lloyd asked as he slipped his gun from the scabbard.

"Probably to a pasture not too far from here. Con Blomberg doesn't own much land in these parts in spite of his wealth. Most of his property is back east or rented out. Now, let's spread out and ride with extra caution."

With guns held in readiness, the seven men rode down the small descent and up the farther incline. Many trees and bushes growing near the top of the hill offered cover for them until they reached the final ridge, then ended abruptly a few yards beyond. Cresting the top of the hill, Norman could hear the sound of voices.

As Minuet neared the edge of the trees, Norman only had time to notice a few men standing near a corral, three saddled and tired looking mounts, and a few cattle behind the fence before a cry warned everyone of the approaching riders. A shot rang out and whistled past Norman's hat as Minuet, startled, gave a sudden step sideways.

"Get off this land," a voice shouted. "You're trespassin'!"

"Throw down your guns," Mr. Mavrich shouted back. "You're all under arrest for cattle stealing."

The only answer to that was more gun fire which the men from Triple Creek returned from the shelter of the trees.

Norman soon had his hands full with Minuet, for the young mustang, having never been under gunfire, was terrified, and plunged and reared trying to break away. After emptying his rifle, Norman traded it for his handgun, talking soothingly to his horse the while.

At last, shouting for his men to hold their fire, for he saw that several of the rustlers had been wounded or were dropping their guns in surrender, Mr. Mavrich dismounted and, with gun still in hand, led Minuet over to the corral.

"Get your hands up and line up along this fence. All of you!" Norman barked.

As the surrendering men moved to obey, the Triple Creek hands rode up and, while some covered the prisoners, the others began tying them up. No one was seriously hurt, but Norman noticed that Blomberg and Shy Adams were not among them. Suddenly hearing Bruce's voice, he turned.

"Well, Mr. Bishop, I thought you'd have more hands out today."

"Bruce!" the man exclaimed in surprise. "What are you doing here?" His voice changed and he snarled, "Turning traitor, are you? Just wait! If Shy doesn't do you in, I promise you, I will."

Bruce seemed unmoved and finished tying his man securely. "It seems you should have been a little more careful of who you hired, Bishop. I don't think Blomberg is going to be happy with this arrangement. Not one bit. Now you can just sit right there and wait." Seeing that the rest of the disgruntled men were tied, Bruce sprang into the corral and strode towards the cattle which were bunched up on the farther side by the fence.

"Mavrich, take a look at this."

CHAPTER 24

SETTLING SCORES

Norman, having issued some low instructions to the rest of his men, glanced over to where his friend was inspecting the cattle. Holstering his gun, he vaulted into the corral and hurried across the ground. "What is it, Bruce?"

"Does this look like a rebrand to you?" Bruce pointed to the hide of the nearest cow.

After a quick examination, Norman nodded. "Sure does. It wasn't done very well either. They tried to make that C into an O but it doesn't match up any too well. Huh, and take a look at the T. Whoever was doing this branding sure had trouble lining things up." Together the two men moved in among the cattle, inspecting the brands. There were about a dozen in the corral and each had been rebranded. Some brands were done better than others leaving an almost believable I-O on the hides, but most were dead giveaways of rebranding.

"Hmm," Bruce mused aloud, taking off his hat and scratching his reddish-blond hair, "I-O. I think they left off one letter of the new brand."

Turning questioning eyes on his friend, Norman raised his eyebrows. "What letter?"

"U—This brand should be I-O-U for stealing your cattle."

Norman snorted and shook his head with a grim smile.

Edmund Bruce always managed to see humor in things when no one else could. "Well, let's leave these cattle and start a search for Blomberg, Adams, and the rest of the stock. I hope they haven't rebranded them too."

A sudden shout alerted the two men, and they whirled quickly. Alden was already in the saddle and urging Strawberry Girl into a gallop while others pointed towards the old weather-beaten barn.

Norman took one look and broke into a run. Reaching the fence he leapt over it and snatched Minuet's reins. "Bruce, take charge here!" His shout was flung over his shoulder as he hit the saddle on the run. Leaning forward he urged, "Come on, girl."

Minuet needed no urging. All day she had been eager to fly over the ground, but Norman had always held her back. Now he wanted speed, and she gave it to him. The ground seemed to melt away under her hooves, and the gap between Norman and Alden was closing rapidly. But Norman wasn't even looking at his ranch hand, his focus was on Con Blomberg, the man reported to be behind the entire cattle rustling operation and the one who had insulted his sister in the streets of Rough Rock.

As the fleet mustang came abreast of Alden's quarter horse, Norman shouted, "Head back to the others. I'll take care of Blomberg!" Then he leaned low over Minuet's neck again.

Racing along, Norman wondered where Blomberg was going or if he was just trying to get away. "I wonder how long of a chase he'll give us," he mused. "His horse seems pretty fresh, but no matter how long it takes we'll catch him, won't we, girl?"

The gap between the two riders slowly began to close. Several times already Blomberg had looked behind him and then slapped his horse with the ends of the reins, trying to urge him to faster speeds. It was no use. After another mile, Blomberg's horse began to visibly slacken his pace. As Minuet neared the tiring horse, Blomberg turned with his gun in his hand and started firing at the approaching rider, but his shots were wild. Before Blomberg had time to reload, Norman was upon him and, leaning over, tugged him from the saddle, almost landing on top of him in the dust. Quickly springing up, he jerked the other man to his feet.

"Con Blomberg, I have a few scores to settle with you."

Blomberg doubled up his fists. "I ain't afraid of you, Mavrich," he snarled. For once he wasn't drunk. "An' I'll teach you a lesson for meddlin' in my affairs."

"I think you are in need of one on how to treat my sister." Norman's voice was low and his eyes were flashing steel.

Although Blomberg was a shade taller and many pounds heavier than his opponent, Norman had fought the bully before and knew his weakness. The years of idle living, much drinking and little exertion had left Blomberg short of wind for any struggle. Keeping his wits about him, Norman blocked the first blow and delivered one to Blomberg's midsection causing the man to stagger back a few steps. Careful to keep out of his opponent's heavier but poorly aimed swings, he moved in and out, skillfully keeping up steady blows which left Blomberg constantly retreating, gasping for breath. As the big bully continued moving backwards, his foot came down in a small dip in the earth and he twisted and began to fall.

Instantly Mavrich leapt forward and, gripping him by the front of the shirt, delivered a solid uppercut to the man's unshaven jaw. Blomberg dropped like a stone and lay unmoving in the dirt.

For a moment, Norman Mavrich let him lie there. "Now get up," he snapped. "I'm taking you in."

"I'll have . . . the law . . . on you . . . Mavrich!" Blomberg threatened, wheezing for breath.

"Right now I am the law," Norman replied. "And you are under arrest for cattle stealing." He gave a whistle and Minuet trotted over to him. Snatching a piece of rope from the saddle, he ordered, "Now get to your feet, Blomberg."

When the man didn't move quickly enough, he was dragged roughly up and ordered to drop his gun belt. With shaking hands, Blomberg did as he was directed and then, following his captor's instructions, mounted his horse.

"Don't even think of trying to escape," Norman said, as he tied his prisoner's hands firmly to the pommel. "You wouldn't get far on foot or on your horse." He was right. Blomberg's horse was exhausted and all the fight seemed to have gone out of Blomberg.

Having retrieved the gun belt from the ground, Norman took the reins of Blomberg's horse, swung up on Minuet, and they headed back the way they had come.

There was a shout of welcome when Norman rode up with his prisoner some time later. The sun was well down in the west and it would be dark in another few hours.

"We've nearly got them all, Mavrich," Hardrich greeted his boss, taking the reins of Blomberg's mount. "Sheriff's already taken most of 'em off to jail."

Dismounting, Norman slapped Minuet's neck affectionately and said, "Sheriff's been here?"

"Yep. He was riding out here today to do a little checking and came upon us. Once Bishop saw it was all over, he started talking."

Two of the men came over and took charge of Blomberg while Scott took the weary horses, leaving Mr. Mavrich and his foreman a chance to talk.

"What about Shy? And were any of our men hurt?"

Hardrich shook his head. "No, besides a few scratches our men came off fine. No one knows where Shy Adams is though. We came upon a few men guarding Triple Creek cattle back in the pasture. They were all sitting by a fire and not a shot was fired. I had Burns, Barker and Tracy hidden with their rifles while I rode up to the men asking for information. I didn't recognize any of them and it was all over in a few minutes. They told us they had heard shots coming from the ranch buildings and that Shy had ridden off in that direction, but no one here has seen him."

"Think he took off?" Norman questioned.

Kicking a clump of dirt with the toe of his boot, Hardrich shook his head slowly. "Hard telling. He could have, but—" He shrugged.

Bruce had joined the two men as Hardrich was finishing his story. "Shy isn't much of a cattle man, but he likes money, so he could be waiting around to see if Blomberg shows up. He's going to want to be paid."

"I reckon you're right there," Norman nodded. "But the question is, where is Shy now?"

In silence the three men stood watching the activity going on around them. Scott was cooling off Minuet and Blomberg's horse. St John was making coffee and Tracy was guarding Blomberg.

Noticing the absence of most of his men, Mr. Mavrich asked, "Where are the others?"

"I sent Barker, Tompkins and Greg back with the Sheriff, to take the prisoners to jail. Alden, Maynard, Burns, Hearter and Wilson are bringing our cattle in from the farther pasture."

St. John called that the coffee was ready and the men sauntered over. Shadows were lengthening as Norman finished his. It would be dark in another hour. "I'd best be getting back to the ranch before Jenelle gets too worried, and there's no telling what Davis will try to do."

"But," Bruce protested, "you left Doc there, didn't you?"

"Yep. But only until Carmond could come over and keep a watch on Ky. Hardrich," Norman turned to his foreman. "I think I'll take Bruce and . . ." he thought a moment. "Well, I reckon that'll be it. St. John can stay and cook, you might need Scott, Tracy's watching Blomberg and the others are gone.

"I'd leave Bruce here, but I could use another hand to take care of chores. Do you know if the sheriff is coming back tonight?"

"Thought he was."

"Well, there's no use taking Blomberg with us if Sheriff Hughes is coming back here. Bruce, you ready to go?"

Gulping down the last of his coffee, Norman's friend replied, "Soon's I saddle up Dakota."

In less than ten minutes the two men were riding towards Triple Creek Ranch by way of the main roads. Their pace was steady and neither man spoke much. The ride in the light of the setting sun was peaceful and the events of the past hours seemed almost like a dream.

"I'm glad that's over," Norman sighed. "I've got a ranch to run."

As Norman and Edmund Bruce dismounted before the barn on Triple Creek, the kitchen door was flung open spilling a stream of light across the dark yard.

"Norman?"

"Yep, Sis, I'm back," Norman called to the figure on the porch.

The next minute Orlena flew across the yard to fling her arms about her brother exclaiming, "Did you catch them? We were worried about you. Did you really get them all? Where are the others? What happened? Oh, Norman!"

Tired though he was, Norman hugged his sister tightly and laughed. "Tell Jenelle and Mrs. O'Connor I'll be in as soon as I can, but we're all fine."

"But what—"

"Run along! I'll tell you all about it when I come in."

"Promise?"

Undoing the cinch, Norman promised, adding, "And ask Mrs. O'Connor to have a plate ready for Mr. Bruce."

Seeing that Norman wouldn't tell her anything more then, Orlena hurried back to the house.

Having already unsaddled Dakota, Bruce reached for Minuet's bridle. "Here, let me finish this. You should head to the bunkhouse and check on Davis."

"Thanks. I'll do that."

Moments later, when Mr. Mavrich stepped into the quiet bunkhouse, he was greeted by a relieved Alex Carmond who rose from his chair quickly. "I thought sure something had happened to you," he remarked quietly. "Did you catch 'em?"

Mavrich nodded. "Yep. How're Davis and Ky?"

"Ky hasn't been any trouble. He just lies there quiet, hardly eats or moves. Now Davis," and the rancher from the Running C shook his head as he glanced over to the bunk where the man lay. "He's been restless. I had the hardest time keeping him in bed the past few hours. Wanted to head after you and lend a hand in catching the rustlers. He just dropped off to sleep about thirty minutes ago. But I'm mighty glad you're back. Where are the rest of your men?"

Briefly Norman filled him in on what had taken place, and hardly had he finished when the door of the bunkhouse opened and Bruce stepped inside. He carried a plate of food.

"I reckon you can head over to the house now whenever you want, Mavrich," Bruce remarked, setting down his plate and dropping his hat on a chair, but looking at Mr. Carmond.

Realizing that neither man had been introduced, Norman nodded from one to the other. "Bruce, this is Alex Carmond from the Running C. Carmond, Edmund Bruce, friend from my college days."

The two men shook hands. Then Carmond said, "Well, Mavrich, glad to know you're home safe. I'd best be getting back to my own ranch before my wife gets the men into a search party for me."

"Thanks for taking over for me here, Carmond."

The rancher put his hat on and stepped outside, saying, "Anytime, Mavrich. You'd have done the same thing for me."

After a few words with Bruce, Norman hurried to the ranch house. He was hungry and he wanted to see Jenelle. To his surprise, he discovered her sitting in her rocking chair in the dining room.

"Jenelle!" he exclaimed, stepping quickly across the

room to greet her with a kiss. "What are you doing down here?"

Jenelle laughed lightly. "Surely you didn't expect me to stay in bed the rest of my life, did you. Marian will be ten days old tomorrow, and Dr. French said I could come down tonight if I felt up to it. Now, do sit down and eat, dear, before your supper grows cold."

Norman needed no urging, for the plate Mrs. O'Connor set before him made him realize just how hungry he was. Half way through his meal, he remarked, "You know, I was so busy today that I never did stop to eat. And, come to think of it," Norman paused with his fork almost to his lips, "not one of the men even mentioned eating."

"Norman Mavrich," Jenelle scolded, "how could you ride your men all day without anything to eat? I do hope they had something tonight."

"Uh huh, That's why I left St. John with them. He'll cook up something tasty." And he returned to his meal.

Orlena was growing impatient. At last she could wait no longer. "Norman, what happened? How did you catch the rustlers? Didn't anyone get hurt? How did you know they were the rustlers? When—"

"Whoa!" Norman held up his hand with a grin. "Slow down, Sis. If you'll pour me another glass of water, I'll tell you the whole story."

The following morning Norman went out to the bunkhouse. He wanted to talk with Ky and see how Davis was doing. He found them both awake; the one silent and withdrawn, the other restless.

"Morning, Davis," Norman greeted the injured ranch hand.

"Mavrich, did ya catch 'em?" Davis tried to sit up, but fell back under the pressure of a firm hand.

"Mack Davis," Norman scolded, "lie still. That wound you got was no light thing. Now you stay down on that pillow until Doc says you can get up, or I'll hog tie you to the bed."

A hearty burst of laughter from the other side of the room, caused both ranch hand and ranch boss to look up.

"Sorry," Bruce chuckled, "but I was just remembering the time you hog tied me to the bed when I said I'd run off and join the army, Mavrich." He laughed again. "You wouldn't untie me until I promised I'd finish school first."

Norman chuckled. "The things you remember." He shook his head.

Davis grinned and promised, "I'll stay here. But I reckon I'd rest better knowin' if ya got them rustlers."

Taking the hint, Norman pulled up a chair and launched into a brief account of catching the thieves.

Davis listened intently. "Now what'll ya do with Ky?" he asked softly.

CHAPTER 25

TYING UP LOOSE ENDS

Norman turned and looked over at the bunk where the man Davis had caught lay staring at the wall, his face expressionless. "I don't know yet." He rose. Bruce had left the bunkhouse while Mr. Mavrich was talking, leaving the ranch boss alone with Davis and the wounded rustler. "Get some rest now, Davis," Norman instructed quietly before crossing the room to the other occupied bunk.

Ky didn't turn his head when Mr. Mavrich approached, but Norman saw him swallow hard.

"How are you feeling this morning, Ky?" Norman's voice was low and kind.

There was no answer.

"Is your leg bothering you?"

A faint shake of the head was the only answer.

"Would you like some water?"

When no answer or response came, Norman placed a chair next to the bed and sat down. For several minutes he looked at the man, saying nothing, but praying for wisdom. The more he studied the man's face, the more youthful it seemed. A dark beard covered the chin and hid the cheekbones from sight giving the impression of age, but there was something about the eyes that contradicted the rough look the beard gave.

"Ky, would you like to shave and clean up a bit?"

The question was so sudden and unexpected that the man turned and stared. His eyes dropped quickly but he muttered, "Reckon I would."

After helping him up and bringing a basin of water, soap and a razor, Norman left Ky alone and busied himself with other things about the bunkhouse often neglected during the busy times when ranch work was pressing. As he worked, he wondered what would happen to Blomberg. "His place could be made into a nice ranch or farm if someone were to take care of it," he mused. "Tompkins has been looking for a place to start his own ranch now that he's got several young ones. But I'd better not suggest anything until I know what's going to happen."

Looking in on Ky a quarter of an hour later, Norman paused in the doorway. The man called Ky was gone; in his place, leaning back against the wall looking exhausted, was a young man. He couldn't be more than nineteen, Norman guessed, for he appeared to be about the same age as Lloyd. What was this boy doing mixed up with rustlers?

Quietly crossing the room, he asked softly, "Do you feel better?"

Ky opened his eyes. "Yes, sir. Thank you." He spoke almost timidly and kept his eyes down.

After helping him back to bed, Norman sat down beside him and asked, "Are you ready to talk?"

"I suppose I should." He fumbled with a loose button and continued, "My real name is Kyle James. I didn't want to work with the rustlers, honest Mr. Mavrich, but he made me."

"Who?"

"My uncle, the one who calls himself Cass Bishop, this time."

"This time?" Norman raised his eyebrows. "You mean he goes by other names? Has he been rustling cattle long?"

The boy nodded. "He uses a different name each place we work. And it's always cattle rustling, but he's never been caught before. I didn't want to help him," he repeated, "but he said I had no choice. Mother's been sick, and Uncle sends my cut of the pay back to the house. At least he says that's what he does."

"How long have you been working with your uncle, Kyle?"

"A little over a year, sir."

"Do you rustle cattle all the time?"

"No, sir, only when we can find someone who'll pay to have it done. Other times I find odd jobs in the towns we stop in. I don't know what Uncle does then. Unless we're working with cattle, he pretty much lets me alone, if he's not drunk."

Norman was silent a moment and then asked, "Who taught you to use your gun?"

"Pa did a little before he died, but I'm not a good shot. That was just a lucky one that hit your man."

"Tell me Kyle, what did you do before you started working for your uncle?"

Kyle turned his face away and lay still for a few minutes. "I tried to run our small ranch, but rustlers took our cattle and then Uncle came and talked Mother into sending me with him. But I think he's the one who stole the cattle!" He turned back a flushed face. "I can't prove a thing, Mr. Mavrich, but someone did and soon after the last ones disappeared, Uncle came riding up."

"Why didn't you go to the sheriff?"

"I couldn't. The sheriff was gone, and his deputy was related to another rancher who had been trying to buy our lands and cattle for over a year." He shook his head. "The only thing I could do was go with Uncle. I didn't know at the time what his work was, and I'm sure Mother didn't either. But now . . ." His voice trailed off, and he rubbed his thumbs over the blanket. "I suppose you have to turn me over to the law."

"Well, I'll have a talk with the sheriff. No doubt your uncle has told all about your part in the business. I'm not sure if there's anything I can do, but I'll look into it. Now, will you give me your word that you won't leave this place without my permission?"

The young man's eyes raised and met the keen grey ones above him. "I give you my word, Mr. Mavrich." He blinked quickly, but a tear escaped and trickled down his cheek. "I didn't—" He stopped and swallowed hard. "I didn't think anyone would ever trust me again. Thank you, sir!"

A firm pressure of the hand was all Norman answered, but it seemed enough to the young man, for he gave a long sigh, relaxed and closed his eyes.

"That poor lad!" Bruce exclaimed after Norman finished telling Kyle's story. "You think he's telling the truth?"

"I'm sure of it; you would be too if you heard him."

Bruce nodded. "I've never known you to be wrong when it comes to a man's character, but what are you going to do now?"

Norman sighed. "I reckon I'll ride into town and have a talk with the sheriff."

"Speaking of the sheriff," Bruce commented, pulling his gloves from his back pocket, "I wonder why Ky never went and told any sheriff or anyone else about his uncle."

"I get the feeling he's rather timid and doesn't know who to trust anymore. He needs help." Norman shook his head. "But I should be off for town and that talk with the sheriff." He led Apache from the barn and prepared to mount him. "Cattle rustlers, a lad who needs help, spring round-up—I tell you, Ned, this is almost as hard as college finals."

"Then you shouldn't have any trouble," Bruce laughed. "What do you want me to do while you're gone?"

"I expect the men will be bringing the cattle back later on today. Can't hurry cattle, but I want them put in the nearest pasture." And Norman pointed to the distant fence line marking the edge of it. "It'd be a waste of time to turn them loose only to round them up next week. Besides, they might be needed. Haven't had time to ride fence on it yet . . ."

"Consider it done. Anything else?"

Norman shook his head. "Just keep an eye on Davis and Kyle now and then. I imagine Greg and Tompkins will be along any time now unless they rode out to Blomberg's place thinking we were all still there. If they show up, we still have to check the corrals and get everything ready for spring round-up."

Riding Apache along the road to town a little later, Norman Mavrich gazed over the wide, grassy ranch lands towards the distant mountains. The sun was bright and warm, piles of featherbed clouds lay stacked on the southern horizon while the rest of the deep blue sky was clear. Tipping his head back, Norman caught sight of an eagle soaring far above and smiled at the sound of a meadowlark singing gaily from the top of a fencepost.

His leisurely musing came to an abrupt halt when he reached Rough Rock, however; for a crowd of men and women thronged the main street before the sheriff's office and the jail, all talking at once.

"What's going on?" Norman asked the closest man.

"Mavrich! He tried to rob the saloon, but he made a mess of things and the sheriff got him! I guess that's the last of the rustlers around here, eh?"

"I missed something there, Rogers; who tried to rob the saloon?"

"Don't know his name, but I reckon the sheriff does. Say, you ought to know, you're the one who rounded up the rest of them loose-fingered desperadoes. What was it like? Did they put up a big fight? Hey, folks, here's Mavrich!"

Sensing that he would be besieged by folks clambering for yesterday's story if he remained there, Mr. Mavrich skirted the crowd and dismounted before the sheriff's office. After tying Apache to the hitching post, he stepped up to the porch and opened the door, glad to get away from the noisy throng.

Sheriff Hughes and Deputy Travis looked up as

Norman entered. "Mavrich," the sheriff greeted, holding out his hand. "Fine work you and your men did yesterday."

"Thank you, but what's all the excitement?"

"You haven't heard? Shy Adams tried to rob the saloon last night and Travis and I brought him in."

"Well," Norman nodded. "I believe that wraps up the last of the rustlers."

"Not quite," Travis corrected. "According to Cass Bishop, there's still another one loose. He's the one who's been taking your cattle."

Resting one foot on a chair, Norman leaned an elbow on his knee and nodded. "Kyle James; we've had him since Friday."

"What?" Travis exclaimed while the sheriff added,

"You sure can keep a secret, Mavrich."

Norman shrugged. "I didn't think it wise to let the others know we had one of their men; it might have spoiled our plans. But, Sheriff, I want to have a talk with you about Kyle."

"Sure thing. Travis, send those people out there on about their business. The middle of the street isn't a town hall."

Travis departed, and Norman took a seat.

"And that's all I know. What do you think, Sheriff?" Norman crossed one booted foot over his knee and looked across the desk at Sheriff Hughes. He had just finished telling his story of Kyle James.

Leaning back thoughtfully in his chair, the sheriff frowned. "Frankly, Mavrich, I don't know what to tell you. He was stealing cattle—"

"I'm not pressing any charges against him."

"But there are other places he did it. I think, now mind me I'm not certain this will work, but I think, if he were willing to tell everything he knows about the other thefts, the judge might drop any charges. Bishop is willing to tell all about this one, placing all the blame on Blomberg, of course, but I doubt he'll even mention the other places. Do you think young Kyle would confess everything?"

"Yes, I think he would, if he knew he could leave his uncle."

"Good. I already sent word to the judge and the marshall. Are you keeping the stolen cattle separate from the rest of your stock?"

Norman nodded. "I thought I would until this thing is settled."

"I saw some of those rebrands," the sheriff shook his head, "and I must say, they were some of the worst—"

The door opened and Deputy Travis came in. "Sorry to interrupt, Sheriff, but this telegram just arrived for you." He handed a slip of paper to the sheriff who opened and read it at once.

"Ah, the judge should be arriving tonight, and we should be able to get this whole thing settled before the end of the week."

Standing, Norman picked up his hat. "That's good because I've got a round-up that is almost over due and I was hoping to be ready to start it next week. But I must be going. Sheriff, Travis." He shook hands with each one and then paused with his hand on the door. "By the way, Sheriff, am I relieved of being a deputy yet? I can't keep chasing bad guys for you; I've got a ranch to run."

Sheriff Hughes laughed. "I'd relieve you, Mavrich, but I'd better not until after the judge rules, since you do have one of the rustlers in your custody."

T

The trial took place the following day and the marshall arrived around noon to take Shy Adams away. Since Kyle James was willing to testify against his uncle, and gave the authorities detailed information about the other ranches where they had rustled cattle, the marshall took Cass Bishop away as well. Blomberg, as the one who had hired everyone, received a long prison sentence, while the other men involved received lighter sentences or fines. These men were taken away the following Monday to another prison to serve their terms. As for Kyle, the judge listened to his story and, with a stern warning against mixing with unprincipled men again, released him into the custody of Norman Mavrich until such a time as he could return to his mother.

"Is that what you had in mind?" Bruce asked his friend as they unhitched the wagon back at the Triple Creek when everything was over.
"What, about Kyle?"
Bruce nodded.
"Well, not exactly, but I figure we could use another hand for a while, since Davis isn't going to be riding for a few weeks yet, and it won't hurt him any to learn a little more about ranch life before going back and starting over. And working here a while might help him learn to stand on his own feet." The horses taken care of, Norman leaned back against the doorframe and folded his arms. "What are you planning on doing now that the rustlers have been caught?"
"Oh," Bruce pulled up a piece of grass and began chewing on it. "I reckon if I could find a ranch around these parts that needs an extra hand for a while, I'd stick around. I can ride and rope and I'm not afraid of cattle." He grinned slyly.
Norman laughed and slapped his shoulder. "You're hired. Now come on in. Mrs. O'Connor and Orlena should have supper about ready. Tomorrow night we'll all eat in the bunkhouse as we plan the round-up, but tonight it's just family in the house, and you'll finally get to meet Marian Rebekah."

The evening sun was casting a rosy glow about Triple Creek Ranch. On the porch the Mavrich family were gathered with Mrs. O'Connor and Edmund Bruce. The evening twitter of the birds in the trees and the sound of a fiddle coming from the bunkhouse gave a feeling of peace to those enjoying the brilliant sunset on the western horizon. A soft creak came from the rocking chair where Jenelle was gently rocking baby Marian Rebekah. For once, Mrs. O'Connor sat in another chair with her hands folded in her lap and no knitting or mending to be seen. On the steps, with her elbows on her knees and her chin in her hands, sat Orlena, her dark curls blowing softly in the light breeze which had sprung up.

"I'm glad we don't have to catch rustlers every day," she remarked with a peaceful sigh.

Norman understood her remark and smiled. "Yep, but we'll keep our guard up because they could come again."

Silence fell over the group and then Mr. Bruce, who had been leaning against a post, turned. "I know spring round-up is next, but what comes after that?"

Norman gave a short laugh. "Everyday life on the ranch, I hope."

"Sounds dull," Bruce remarked, though his eyes twinkled.

It was Jenelle's turn to laugh. "If you'll stay around here long enough, you'll find that it's anything but dull. Right, Dear? . . . Norman?"

"Huh?" Norman turned and looked down at his wife. "What was that? I'm afraid I was already planning the round-up."

And now, a sneak preview of Book Four in the
Triple Creek Ranch series:

Inside the fence, Mr. Mavrich and Stephen were waiting, while in the next corral, Scott and Ky were saddling up one of the horses brought in earlier. The rest of the men pressed around the outsides of corral, reserving a spot in the shade for Mrs. Mavrich and Orlena. All were anxious to see how well the new hand could ride. Though he had boasted that he had ridden every horse on the last ranch he worked at, many of the men were doubtful.

"Think he can stay on any horse but Anything?" Alden asked in low tones.

St. John and Burns, the only men within hearing shrugged.

"We'll soon find out," St. John answered. "Look, Scott's bringing Cheyenne; he's almost as steady and old as Anything."

"If the boy doesn't try anything funny," Burns added.

Having saddled the horse with the smallest saddle the ranch owned, Scott led the horse into the corral.

"He's kinda small," Stephen remarked, eying his mount skeptically.

"He's an Indian pony," Mr. Mavrich replied, smiling. "He may be getting along in years, but he still has spirit in him. Take the reins and mount up."

Taking the reins from Scott, Stephen asked, as he looked the pony over, "What's his name?"

"Cheyenne."

Quickly Stephen mounted the small horse and then looked at the ranch boss.

"Walk him around a few time," Norman motioned, stepping into the center of the corral. "Get the feel of the saddle and the horse's gait. That's it. Good. Now try a canter."

It was obvious that the boy at least had been on a horse before for he didn't bounce all over.

"Now slow him down to a walk again," Mr. Mavrich called after Stephen had ridden a few times around the corral.

Stephen tried to obey, but at his firm jerk on the reins, the horse pulled up short and Stephen, unprepared, found himself landing in the dust. Scrambling to his feet, the boy brushed his pants off and cast a half frightened, half defiant look at the spectators and then at Mr. Mavrich.

"You all right?" Mr. Mavrich hadn't moved from his place as he watched Stephen get up. At the boy's nod, he teased gently, "What happened? I told you to walk him, not go flying off his back?" He grinned. "I should have warned you that Cheyenne has a very soft mouth and only needs a slight touch to slow him down." He placed a friendly hand on the boy's shoulder. "Let's try a couple more. Scott, turn Cheyenne into the pasture and saddle Moonlight."

"Yes, sir." And Scott led the pony from the corral.

Within ten minutes the new horse was being led out by Ky. Moonlight was a larger horse and bobbed his head as Stephen scrambled up into the saddle and took the reins. Watching closely, it didn't take Norman long to tell Stephen to pull up and dismount. "This one isn't right for you, son," he remarked, taking the reins as Stephen slid off. "We'll try a few more. Scott, let's try Regina next."

About the Illustrator

Nikola Belley is a self-taught artist, who enjoys exploring various mediums, from sketching to oil painting. A homeschool graduate, she is also a costume designer and seamstress and participates in international folk dance, music studies, and a myriad of family activities. Nikola lives in Missouri with her parents and eight siblings.

Made in the USA
Monee, IL
24 July 2021